COSMO*girl!*
QUIZ BOOK
ALL ABOUT YOU

COSMOgirl! QUIZ BOOK
ALL ABOUT YOU

From the Editors of *CosmoGIRL!*

**Hearst Books
A Division of Sterling
Publishing Co., Inc.
New York**

Copyright © 2004 by Hearst Communications, Inc. All rights reserved.

Library of Congress Cataloging-in-Publication Data Available

10 9 8 7 6 5 4 3 2

Book design by Margaret Rubiano

Published by Hearst Books
A Division of Sterling Publishing Co., Inc.
387 Park Avenue South, New York, NY 10016

CosmoGirl! is a trademark owned by Hearst Magazines Property, Inc., in USA, and Hearst Communications, Inc., in Canada. Hearst Books is a trademark owned by Hearst Communications, Inc.

www.cosmogirl.com

Distributed in Canada by Sterling Publishing
C/o Canadian Manda Group, 165 Dufferin Street, Toronto,
Ontario, Canada M6K 3H6

Distributed in Australia by Capricorn Link (Australia) Pty. Ltd.
P.O. Box 704, Windsor, NSW 2756 Australia

Manufactured in China.

ISBN 1-58816-381-4

Photo Credits:

Jessica Backhaus, pg. 62; Colette DeBarros, pg. 6, 7, 72, 76, 86; Jan Willem Dikkers, pg. 10; Vincente DiPaulo, pg. 24; Viki Forshee, pg. 50; Alexie Hay and Justine Parsons, pg. 18; Ellen Jong, pg. 22, 33; Gregory Kramer, pg. 5, 100; Brooke Nipar, pg. 36; Jeff Olson, pg. 88; Andre Passos, pg. 104; Coliena Rentmeester, pg. 42, 80; Water Sassard, pg. 92; Saye, pg. 12, 16, 28, 38, 46, 52, 56, 60, 84, 108; Mei Tao, pg. 68; Jason Todd, pg. 30.

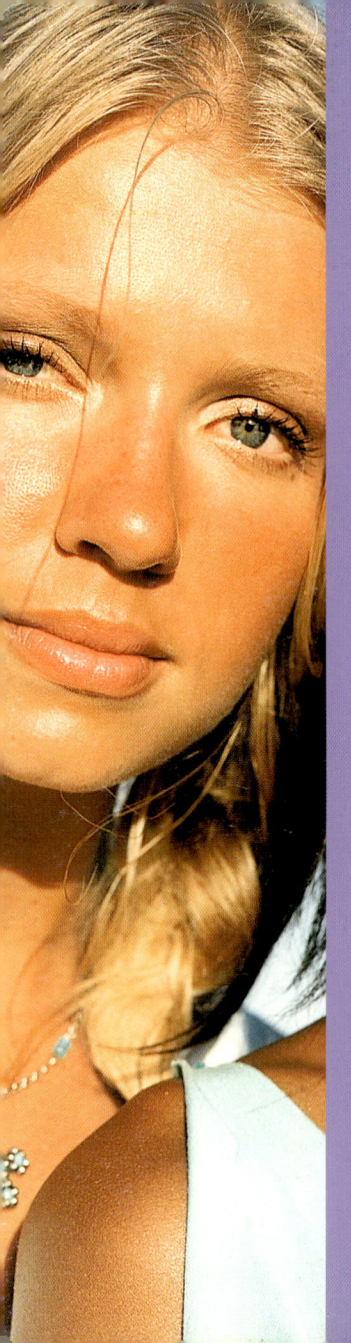

Contents

From Me to You,   8
by Susan Schulz,
Editor in Chief

CosmoGIRL! Fun

Find Your Power Color	13
What Kind of Car Are You?	15
What Kind of Shoe Are You?	19
What Ice Cream Flavor are You?	21
What Decade Do You Belong In?	25
What's Your Internal Weather Report?	27
Do You Have a Sixth Sense?	31
What's Your Metropolitan Match?	33

Inner Girl

What Color is Your Love Life?	39
Why Don't You Have a Boyfriend?	41
Do You Act Your Age?	45

What Kind of Daughter Are You?	49
How Do Guys See You?	53
Attitude Check!	57

Circle of Friends

What Do People Think of You?	63
Find Your Inner Party Animal	69
Are You a Bore?	71
What Kind of Friend Are You?	75
Are You Annoying?	79
Are You a Sucker?	83

Hear Me Roar

Who Runs Your Life?	89
What's Your Secret Power?	93
What's Your Fighting Style?	99
Are You a Goal Getter?	105
Are You a Leader?	109

From Me to You

CosmoGIRL! is all about showing you that you have the power to do whatever you want with your life. That power is within you, and the way I see it, all you need from us at CG! is a little bit of guidance. Think of it like this—we're like the lantern that's leading you through the exciting labyrinth of your life. Along the way there are tons of amazing adventures, and yup, a few pitfalls—but don't worry, because we know where they are and we'll tell you about them before you get to them—so you can safely navigate your way around them and stay on track.

Now, one of *CosmoGIRL*'s favorite ways to help you along this journey of yours is to give you quizzes that let you discover things you may not yet know about yourself. From the letters I get from you at the magazine, you *love* taking quizzes! So in this book, we've gathered a ton of our very best ones.

Grab a pen and take them by yourself, or get together with

some friends and have fun going through them together. I know you'll start to see yourself in insightful (and maybe some crazy?) new ways.

Why do we care so much about helping you "find yourself"? Because you're born to lead, *CosmoGIRL!*, and the better you know yourself, the stronger, more successful, and happier you'll be. That's a pretty good reason, right? Right?! Yeah, we think so.

Let me know what you think of these—and give me ideas for quizzes you'd like to see us do in future issues of *CosmoGIRL!* E-mail me whenever you feel like it—I'm here listening! I'm at <u>susan@cosmogirl.com</u>.

Love,

Susan

CosmoGIRL! fun

FIND YOUR POWER COLOR

Wear it. Write with it. Bathe in it (why not?) for that hit of energy that beats Starbucks any day!

1. Do you write in a journal?
a. Yes, every day.
b. I try, but I'm usually too busy to write it all down.
c. No, but I keep meaning to *start* one.
d. No. Bor-*ring*.

2. What's your favorite kind of movie?
a. An arty film (with subtitles, *s'il vous plaît!*).
b. A total tearjerker drama.
c. A revved-up action adventure flick.
d. A fun (stupid!) comedy.

3. Which airplane seat do you prefer?
a. It just depends on the mood I'm in.
b. A window seat.
c. The aisle, please!
d. Whatever they give me is just fine.

4. Which party game do you like best?
a. Ouija. Break out the board!
b. Truth or Dare.
c. Spin the Bottle. Need an Altoid, anyone?
d. Pictionary.

5. After school, you've got the energy to:
a. Hit the couch for a nap.
b. Just do my homework.
c. Make it through a meeting and practice.
d. Run a marathon, if only I had time.

6. What would you love to do on a Saturday?
a. Hang out in the park and catch up with a friend.
b. Volunteer for a really great cause.
c. Try an extreme sport.
d. Plan a last-minute party.

Add 'em up! Give yourself 1 point for each a, 2 for each b, 3 for each c, and 4 for each d.

6-10 points: Blue You think about things deeply, and you don't mind if your strong opinions make waves. You always know what's right in your *heart*—that's why friends call you in a crisis. But to *keep* that stress away, get blue sheets or an ocean-toned screensaver to create a personal oasis.

11-15 points: Green You're down-to-earth and giving, not to mention supportive, which makes you a great friend. Even *guys* can reveal their problems to you—your ability to talk things through brings out everyone's peaceful side. To maintain *your* inner calm, write on green paper or with green ink.

16-19 points: Red Spontaneous and passionate, you go for the goal, whether it's the lead in a play *or* that cutie in History. But before you give something your all (a guy, a project, whatever), make sure your plan is realistic—it'll save you heartbreak later. And don't *hide* that fiery spirit. Fill up your closet with red accessories.

20-24 points: Yellow Hello, sunshine! You're one successful, smiley chica. Teachers love you, guys trust you, and you've got tons of friends. But remember, it *is* okay to be sad sometimes. Share your troubles with one of those many friends—you'll bounce back fast. Yellow can be hard to *wear,* but use a bright notebook for an energy infusion.

WHAT KIND OF CAR ARE YOU?

1. What's your dream destination?
a. The Colorado Rockies.
b. Hawaii.
c. Paris, but of course!
d. Vegas, baby.

2. Which dare would you take?
a. Running outside in the cold—in my undies!
b. Crank-calling: "Is Mr. Hugh Jass there?"
c. Asking out a stranger.
d. Mooning a passing car.

3. What's your favorite car color?
a. Forest green.
b. Deep blue.
c. Glittery gold.
d. Bright red.

4. Your best friend is having a party. She asks you to:
a. Make the food.
b. Invite people.
c. Decorate her place.
d. Make mix CDs.

5. Makeup is:
a. A pain.
b. Something I don't use much of.
c. A must.
d. Fun to play around with.

6. What's your perfect workout?
a. Hiking.
b. Running.
c. Yoga.
d. Kickboxing.

Add 'em up! Give yourself 1 point for each a, 2 for each b, 3 for each c, and 4 for each d.

6-10 points: Range Rover

Whether you're off-roading or heading to the slopes, there's no challenge you can't handle. You're powerful and capable, and your positive energy is unbeatable. Just be sure to get enough "gas" (food and sleep) so you don't tire out too quickly.

11-15 points: BMW Sedan

You are one well-oiled machine—and you know you don't have to be the flashiest to be the best. You're all about reliability, loyalty, and making other people feel comfortable. Keep using your fabulous common sense and you'll be in great shape for the long run.

16-19 points: Mercedes-Benz Convertible

Every detail about your vehicle rocks. Sophisticated and versatile, you pack more than enough power to get you where you want to go (hint: It's far). Your challenge: Don't worry about little scratches and dings. Learn to sit back and enjoy the ride.

20-24 points: Porsche Carrera

You definitely live life in the fast lane. People get out of your way when you zoom by, and it's a good thing, because there's no stopping you once you get a great idea. But watch those speed limits—just because you can go fast doesn't mean you always should.

WHAT KIND OF SHOE ARE YOU?

Read on to meet your "sole" mate.

1. When someone asks what your favorite class is, you're quick to answer:
a. Sociology.
b. Study hall.
c. Gym.
d. Art.

2. If you had to get to school on just two wheels, you'd prefer to arrive on a:
a. Retro-new Schwinn.
b. Vespa.
c. Mountain bike.
d. Harley.

3. As a kid, your Barbie doll was usually:
a. Dressed impeccably.
b. Making out with Ken.
c. Enclosed in a dusty box under your bed.
d. Sporting a customized punk-rock hairdo.

4. When you get glammed up for a party, you want people to say you look like:
a. Reese Witherspoon.
b. Britney Spears.
c. Katie Holmes.
d. Avril Lavigne.

5. Which of these reality shows would you most want to be on?
a. The Bachelorette
b. The Real World
c. Survivor
d. Fear Factor

6. If you could have just one, which a.m. beverage would you drink?
a. Freshly squeezed o.j.
b. Cappuccino
c. Fruit smoothie
d. Red Bull

Scoring*

mostly a's: classic flat
You always seem poised, even if you have on safety gear in chem lab. That quality, like flats, is timeless—and it's why everyone knows they can always count on you. You know that true grace comes from being true to yourself.

mostly b's: sexy stiletto
For you, there's no dress rehearsal, so you just sashay through life (looking great, we might add!). Risky and to-the-point (à la these heels), you're always ready for your close-up—hey, you want the attention you deserve!

mostly c's: comfy sneaker
Your mission: to do it all. You bounce easily between activities—just like your favorite pair of trainers. There's always another adventure coming, so you'll always have new ways to stay occupied (and happy)!

mostly d's: kick-butt boot
You're brave and will stomp all over convention...if you must. You leave your imprint everywhere, sorta like these thick-soled bad boys! Whether you're making a weird dish in home ec or shopping for clothes, you're always unique.

*End up with a tie? Just pick the description that best fits your personality.

WHAT ICE CREAM FLAVOR ARE YOU?

Listen—this is info you need to know!

1. On a Saturday afternoon, you'd most prefer:
a. Biking in the park.
b. Writing poetry and playing your guitar.
c. Scoping out cute guys at the mall.
d. Shopping with friends.

2. Which of these four female stars do you tend to identify with most?
a. Mandy Moore
b. Alanis Morissette
c. Alicia Keys
d. Gwen Stefani

3. You'd want to be famous for:
a. Saving an endangered species of animal.
b. Being the first female president—better look out, George W.!
c. Designing dresses.
d. Throwing glam parties.

4. What's the one thing in your closet you love the most?
a. My comfy-slash-cute-slash-groovy sneakers.
b. My funky vintage jacket.
c. My sexy leather pants.
d. My funny conversation-starter T-shirt.

5. In school, what subject do you usually get the best grades in?
a. Biology
b. History
c. Art
d. English

6. Your dream guy kind of reminds you of:
a. Andy Roddick (that adorable tennis player)
b. Tobey Maguire
c. Enrique Iglesias
d. Ashton Kutcher

Scoring
If you get a tie, consider yourself swirled!

mostly a's: Vanilla

Even though you're earthy, you're anything but plain. You're perfectly at ease in any situation—whether it's chatting up your boyfriend's mom or passing out Greenpeace flyers to strangers. And you look prettiest when your hair's in a ponytail and you're wearing no makeup.

mostly b's: Coffee

Your intensity gives everyone a buzz, Miss Coffee. You're smart, smart, smart, and you're a natural born leader (politics, anyone?). You like seeing things from lots of different points of view, and you know how to stand up for what you believe in. Is it any wonder you're totally addictive?

mostly c's: Chocolate

Romantic, creative, and passionate, you're definitely chocolatey. You have the ability to make people melt by seeing deep within them—past the superficial stuff, right to the meaningful core. That means you're a girl with great friendships—and very intense loves.

mostly d's: Strawberry

Tangy and refreshing, you live life at a mile a minute. Your friends admire and adore you, and it's easy to see why: They love that you make them laugh and that you're always up for an unpredictable good time.

WHAT DECADE DO YOU BELONG IN?

Vintage is about more than just clothes—it's a way of life, baby!

1. At a party, you're:
a. With your guitar, leading a group sing-along.
b. On the dance floor, shaking your thang.
c. Mingling! Making connections is key.
d. Playing DJ—everyone loves your taste in music.

2. What's so you?
a. A peasant top and cute flip-flops.
b. A one-shoulder top, bootleg pants, and a side order of gold jewelry.
c. A leather mini and an off-the-shoulder top.
d. A little black dress.

3. You'd be happy:
a. On a mountainside, communing with nature.
b. At a coffee shop, flirting with a cute new guy.
c. On a podium, accepting your class presidency.
d. In your room, IM-ing all of your friends.

4. Your absolute dream boyfriend:
a. Signs e-mails, "Peace!"
b. Has all the right clothes and can dance!
c. Is going to Harvard.
d. Cooks, speaks Italian, runs marathons, and has a sensitive side.

5. After college, you'd love to:
a. Join the Peace Corps.
b. Become an edgy fashion designer.
c. Work 100-hour weeks and make millions as an investment banker.
d. Own 100 Starbucks.

6. Which of these songs would you say is your personal motto?
a. "Good Day Sunshine"
b. "Dancing Queen"
c. "Girls Just Want to Have Fun"
d. "If It Makes You Happy"

Scoring

If you get a tie, read both categories that apply to you.

mostly a's: 1960s So maybe you don't actually own love beads, but now that we mention it, you're kind of tempted, right? You belong in the '60s! You're a romantic with a sensitive, soulful side. You care deeply about everything you do, whether it's saving the planet or just making a friend feel loved. You simply radiate positive energy—it's no wonder you belong in the decade of peace, love, and happiness.

mostly b's: 1970s Click your heels three times, and we'll take you home to Studio 54, you little disco diva. Well, we would if we could! You, dancing queen, are the life of any party—especially this little party called Life. Your '70s qualities are obvious off the dance floor too. People love your ability to make even the roughest days fun.

mostly c's: 1980s Just like Madonna (back when she wore bras as outerwear), you know what you want and how to get it. You ooze power, smarts, and strength—and that's why you're perfect for the big-spending, big-time '80s. (But don't worry, that doesn't mean you have to have big hair to match!) You love a challenge—whether it's going Ivy League or flirting with the cutest guy in the room. Go you!

mostly d's: 2000s With your innovative personality and intelligence, you belong right in the fast-track '00s. You may work hard, but you play hard too. Direct the school play? No problem. Organize a poetry reading? Piece of cake. You're a total multi-tasking diva, and you truly understand how to carpe diem.

WHAT'S YOUR INTERNAL WEATHER REPORT?

Get the barometer on your outlook, sister!

1. **When a teacher asks for your parents' number, you just assume:**
a. You're in trouble.
b. It's parent-teacher conference time.
c. She's making sure she has the right info.

2. **Your bangs are growing out. When you pass a mirror, you go:**
a. "Oh, sweet Lord! I need a headband."
b. "Mental note: I've gotta get this cut soon."
c. "I'm so moppet-chic!"

3. **You want to see the Ice Capades; your friends say no way. You end up:**
a. Watching it on TV.
b. Going with your mom. (She's no arts snob.)
c. Dragging your friends.

4. **The girls at the musical tryouts all sing like Mariah. You secretly think:**
a. I have no chance.
b. I'll make the chorus.
c. Hopefully I'll get the lead part!

5. **You get a coupon for a free facial in the mail. You think:**
a. Great. Somebody's telling me I have acne.
b. Hmm, would I have to buy something?
c. Free facial. Yay!

6. **A guy at the arcade looks at you, so you:**
a. Figure he likes your friend and feel ugly.
b. Ask your friend, "Did he just check me out?"
c. Smile and invite him to play air hockey.

Scoring

Mostly A's: **cloudy with possible thunderstorms**

You feel a breeze and assume a hurricane is coming! It's great that you have an emergency shelter in case of disaster—but learn to appreciate the sunny days. Write down what's great about you and ask your friends what they admire about you. Soon you'll see the brighter side of life: Yes, he could like you, you could win the class election, and you do have a chance of winning the lottery!

Mostly B's: **partly cloudy, partly sunny**

Hey, sometimes it will rain on your parade, so you try to remember to play in the raindrops. When sucky things happen—like a breakup, or bad grade—you address them, learn, and move on. You know that if you can stay positive, every day will have at least some good parts!

Mostly C's: **not a cloud in sight**

Chance of rain? What's that? Your ability to see the sun makes people wonder if you've ever gone through a tough time. It's great that you've got such a bright attitude—just pay attention to reality and pack a raincoat (a.k.a. backup plan) so you'll have it on the days when you really do need it. Until then...bask in the warmth!

DO YOU HAVE A SIXTH SENSE?

Find out if you've got special ESP powers just waiting to be developed.

1. Ever wake up just before your alarm?
a. I barely wake up after the alarm's been blaring for ten minutes!
b. Occasionally... but it usually just means I have to pee.
c. Definitely!

2. How often do you experience déjà vu?
a. Never.
b. It's happened once or twice.
c. I could swear you've asked me this before...

3. Do you believe in the power of tarot cards?
a. No more than my old UNO deck.
b. Not really, but they can be insightful.
c. Of course—wanna see my deck?

4. How do you usually make decisions?
a. I think them through, using pros and cons.
b. I base them on logic, unless my heart tells me not to.
c. I go with my gut.

5. Can you finish your friend's sentences?
a. Only when I'm listening to her tell the same story for the 200th time.
b. Now and then.
c. All the time!

6. Ever met someone you felt like you knew?
a. Oh, please—that doesn't happen.
b. Yeah, I think I know what you mean.
c. It was like that when I met my best friend!

Add 'em up! Give yourself 1 point for each a, 2 for each b, and 3 for each c.

6-9 points: Princess of Pragmatism The way you see it, if God meant for you to have a third eye, false lashes would come in packs of three! You're sensible and logical. But don't ignore your inner feelings—they may actually be trying to help. We're not saying to drop your rational sense altogether, but practice listening to your gut: Buy the first candy you're drawn to, even if you've never tried it before; skip a street that gives you the creeps. Soon, you'll see that a sixth sense is a totally practical tool.

10-14 points: Extra Perceptive Your rational side may tell you that you're just a girl with good instincts. But give your intuition some credit—it's real. Next time you've got a dilemma (like a red vs. a black prom dress), try this: Say the sensible option out loud ("The black dress; it's cheaper."). Feel disappointed? You'll know in your heart you want the other—it'll make you happier in the long run. By trusting your instincts and your intellect you'll get the best of both worlds.

15-18 points: Totally Tuned In Who needs a Magic 8-Ball with you around?! You're the type who takes a different road to the mall, only to hear later that there was a huge wreck on your usual route. And when it comes to guys, you can spot a player a mile away. But just because your gut tells you to do something doesn't mean it's always right (otherwise we'd all have hitchhiked to the Korn show). Try making pro and con lists to evaluate risks. But then, you knew we were going to say that, didn't you?

WHAT'S YOUR METROPOLITAN MATCH?

Because every international woman of mystery needs a place to call home.

1. You'd rather get a gift card for a:
a. Psychic reading.
b. Spa day.
c. Beauty makeover.
d. Music store.

2. Which summer program is right for you?
a. A creative writing workshop.
b. An "essentials of pastry" class.
c. A Fortune-500 internship.
d. An outdoor-adventure course.

3. At a party, you'd break the ice with:
a. "Is this song a cover?'
b. "Any hot guys here?'
c. "Where'd you get that shirt?"
d. "Ready to start dancing?"

4. Which sounds like the best school field trip?
a. A hands-on pottery demo.
b. A cool museum.
c. A neighborhood walking tour.
d. One you take on senior-ditch day.

5. What snack would you make for your friends?
a. Veggie chili.
b. Chocolate-covered strawberries.
c. Pizza.
d. Nachos with mango salsa.

6. Your personality is most like that of a:
a. Chinchilla—you're unpredictable!
b. Cat—you love lounging in comfort.
c. Dog—you get excited easily.
d. Shark—who needs sleep?

Scoring

Mostly A's: Prague

Feel that buzz? It's your indie spirit, alive in the city that gave birth to the boho lifestyle. Artists and philosophers flock here—kind of like they do to your living room on Friday nights. No wonder Prague's on your to-visit list.

Mostly B's: Paris

Do we hear violins? A daydreamer like you belongs in the land of romantic ideals. High culture and fab art give you the sense that your chic fantasies have come true.

Mostly C's: New York City

Who hearts NY? You! Crowds, shopping, celebs! Your flash-boom-bang personality is right at home. On the subway or in SoHo, one thing you won't be is bored.

Mostly D's: Rio de Janeiro

Do you ever stop to *rest*? This is the ultimate fun town. Festivals, friendly guys, bare-to-there dress codes, and nonstop dancing make life the party you know it *can* be. Hey, why wear pants when bikini bottoms will do?

Inner Girl

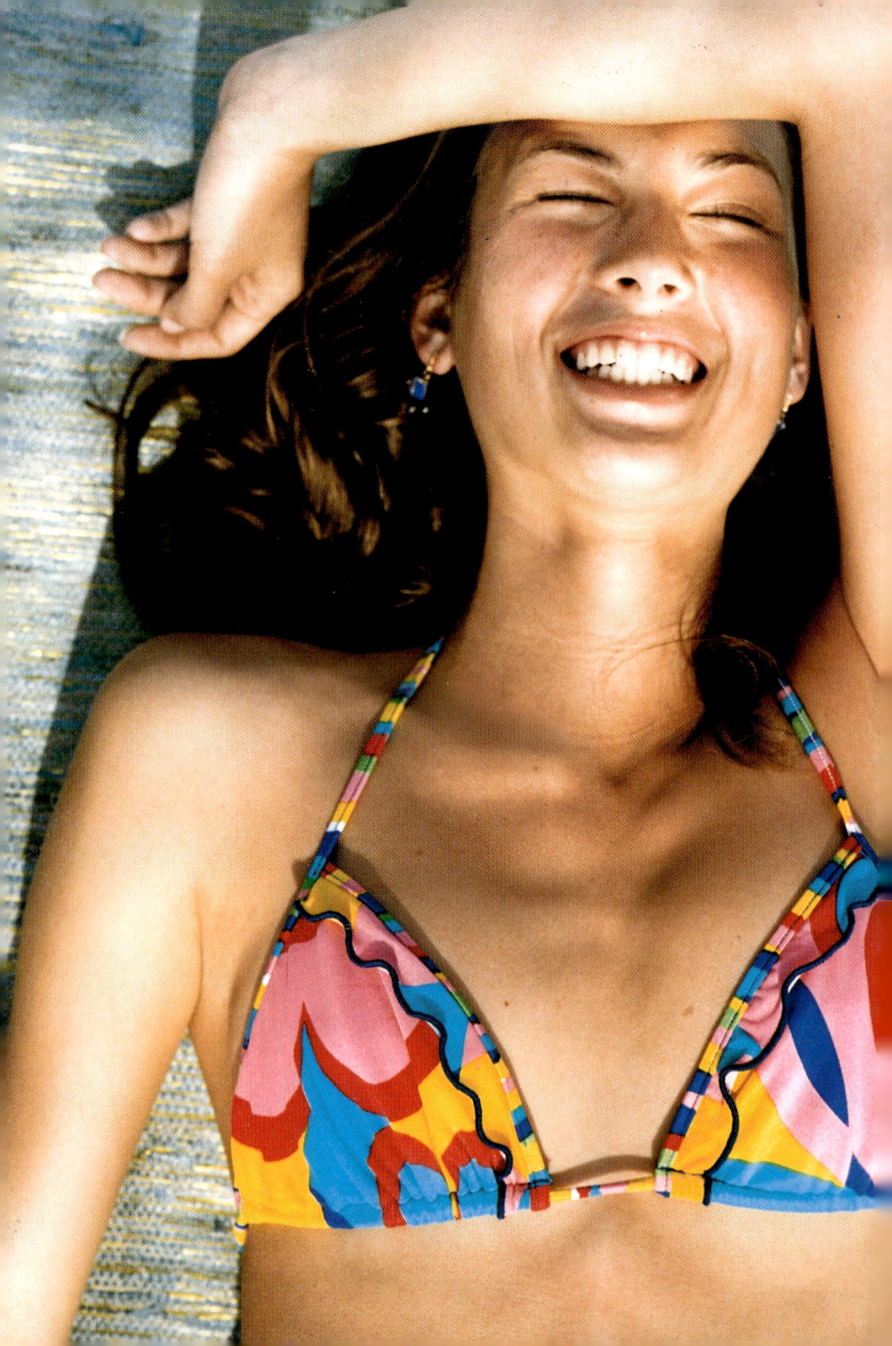

WHAT COLOR IS YOUR LOVE LIFE?

Discover the true hue of your crushing style—red-hot or not!

1. At a dance, you're probably the person:
a. Hanging with your girls.
b. Flirting with different peeps.
c. Dancing thisclose with one guy.

2. Your first question for a love psychic would have to be:
a. "Will I ever get a guy?"
b. "Is he getting serious about me?"
c. "Will he be mine forever?"

3. You get a note from "a secret admirer" and:
a. Go, "psssh"—it's probably one of your friends being ridiculous.
b. Hope it's the guy you like.
c. Giggle and tell your guy thanks.

4. If you're single on Valentine's Day, you:
a. Aren't surprised.
b. Go out with your single friends (and maybe even meet a guy).
c. Get really depressed.

5. When prom time comes, you'll likely go with:
a. Your closest guy friend (he won't mind you gawking at your crush).
b. A cute guy you flirt with at work.
c. Your boyfriend—who else?

6. Major track meet coming up. You're excited to:
a. Check out the events.
b. Warm up with the triple-jumper you've had your eye on.
c. Give your crush a massage.

Scoring

mostly a's: crushing coral
You browse through the grocery store of boys out there at times, but so far, your basket is empty. That's because guys aren't topping your list of priorities right now. Good for you that you're waiting to turn on your fiery side when the right guy catches your eye.

mostly b's: passionate purple
You love love and getting swept off your feet! For you, life right now is about sampling many flavors. But you might be passing up a great guy without even knowing it. Ask friends for outside opinions on your love life if you need some perspective about Mr. Right versus Mr. Right Now. They'll help you know when to get serious.

mostly c's: serious scarlet
Caution: Contents are hot! Deep red is the hue of A Serious Thing, which is what you're always looking for (even if you don't have a special guy at this very instant). When you get involved, you open up your heart and world to that person. That's an amazing quality, and it leads to mature relationships. Red looks great on you!

WHY DON'T YOU HAVE A BOYFRIEND?

Find out why the only tush pocket your hand slips into is your own, cookie!

1. **What do you do when you see that h-o-t soccer player who scored yesterday's winning goal?**
a. Congratulate him on a good game.
b. Playfully pat his cute little butt, guys'-locker-room style.
c. Half smile and kind of look away.

2. **Your older sister takes you to a party while you're visiting her at college. You:**
a. Flirt with some cute guys.
b. Quietly people-watch on the porch.
c. Dance with her and her friends—you came to be with her, after all.

3. **Your parents won't let your sister wear a strapless dress to her prom. You feel bad that she's upset and:**
a. Lobby hard-core on her behalf. Why shouldn't she wear what she wants?
b. Say nothing—why rock the boat?
c. Take her shopping—why not find one she and your parents will like?

4. **The envelope arrives, and—drum roll, please!—you totally rocked your SATs! You:**
a. Bring up your score every chance you get at school the next day.
b. Excitedly tell the people you feel closest to.
c. Tell just your parents—you don't want to rub it in your friends' faces.

41

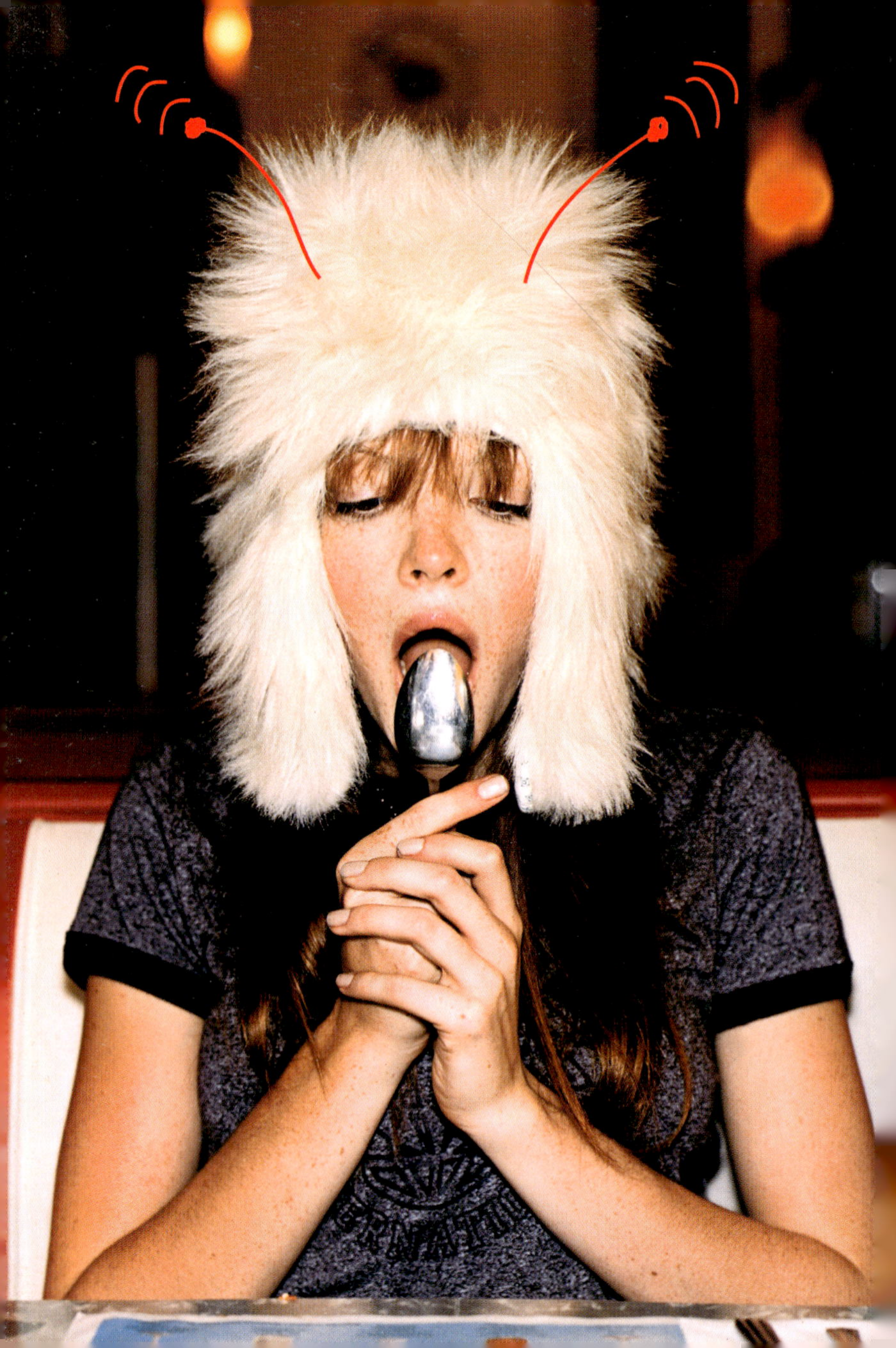

5. **Which best describes what you do when the yearbook comes out at the end of each school year?**

a. Flip through it when you first get it and then lose it in your locker.
b. Carry it in your backpack in case someone asks to sign it.
c. Ask everyone you know to sign it using your funky-colored pens.

6. **You're selling M&Ms for a charity fund-raiser. When you find out your principal is a candy freak, you:**

a. Walk by her office—but then decide not to bother her after all.
b. Schedule a quick visit with her through her secretary.
c. Pop into her office during lunch and give her your best sales pitch.

7. **You have plans to hang out with the girls on Friday night, but your crush calls to ask you to a movie. You:**

a. Say yes—if you say no this time, he might never call again, right?
b. Say yes—your friends know your drop-everything-for-guys rule!
c. Say you can't do it Friday, but how about Saturday instead?

ANSWER KEY:
1: a = 2, b = 3, c = 1;
2: a = 3, b = 1, c = 2;
3: a = 3, b = 1; c = 2;
4: a = 3, b = 2, c = 1;
5: a = 2, b = 1, c = 3;
6: a = 1, b = 2, c = 3;
7: a = 1, b = 3, c = 2

Scoring
Figure out your score to reveal why "us"-ness hasn't come your way—yet.

7-11 points: You're bashful!

You're pretty self-sufficient and are more into doing things one-on-one than in a big group. But lying low means that people (read: guys) may not get to see just how fabulous you are. So start taking small risks every now and then. Next time a cute guy catches your eye, flash that great smile of yours at him and say hi!

12-16 points: You're booked!

You feel secure in yourself, and your friends and interests fill up most of your time. You don't need a guy to make you feel special. But the kind of person who will make you happiest when you're ready will probably be someone who appreciates all of your passions and who has similar interests too.

17-21 points: You're bold!

Amazing opportunities have come to you because you *rarely* back away from what you want! But not all guys are right for your strong personality. Believe it or not, a shy guy might be your best bet—he'll appreciate your take-charge attitude and the fact that you can say *exactly* what you mean.

DO YOU ACT YOUR AGE?

Find out if you belong in a nursery—or a nursing home!

1. **A friend lends you her John Mayer CD on Thursday and asks you to return it on Sunday. You:**
a. Can't find it. But you'll buy her a new one before Sunday.
b. Think it's somewhere in your car; you'll try to make time to find it.
c. Totally flake—you lent it to another friend without thinking.
d. Have it waiting for her at her house, just like you promised.

2. **Mom and Dad have to work late and ask you to get yourself and your kid brother dinner. You:**
a. Chow down on a Twinkie feast and plop in front of the TV.
b. Go through the fridge and whip up turkey burgers and salads.
c. Head to Mickey D's for two quarter pounders—with cheese!
d. Take your brother out to get sandwiches and ice cream.

3. **What did you do with last year's $100 birthday check from Gram and Gramps?**
a. Lost it in your room and asked them if they'd mind writing a new one.
b. Cashed it ASAP and headed to the mall for a shopping spree.
c. Put half in the bank and spent the other $50 on make-up and hair stuff.
d. Deposited it in your savings account so that it could start earning interest.

4. **Your doctor takes the cast off your broken ankle and tells you to wear comfy shoes for a while. You:**
a. Wear nothing but your cushy sneakers for the next month.
b. Wear ballet flats; okay, they're not orthopedic, but they're flat, right?
c. Wear your boots with the small motorcycle heel.
d. Wear your cool high-heel platforms; any other shoe would kill your style.

45

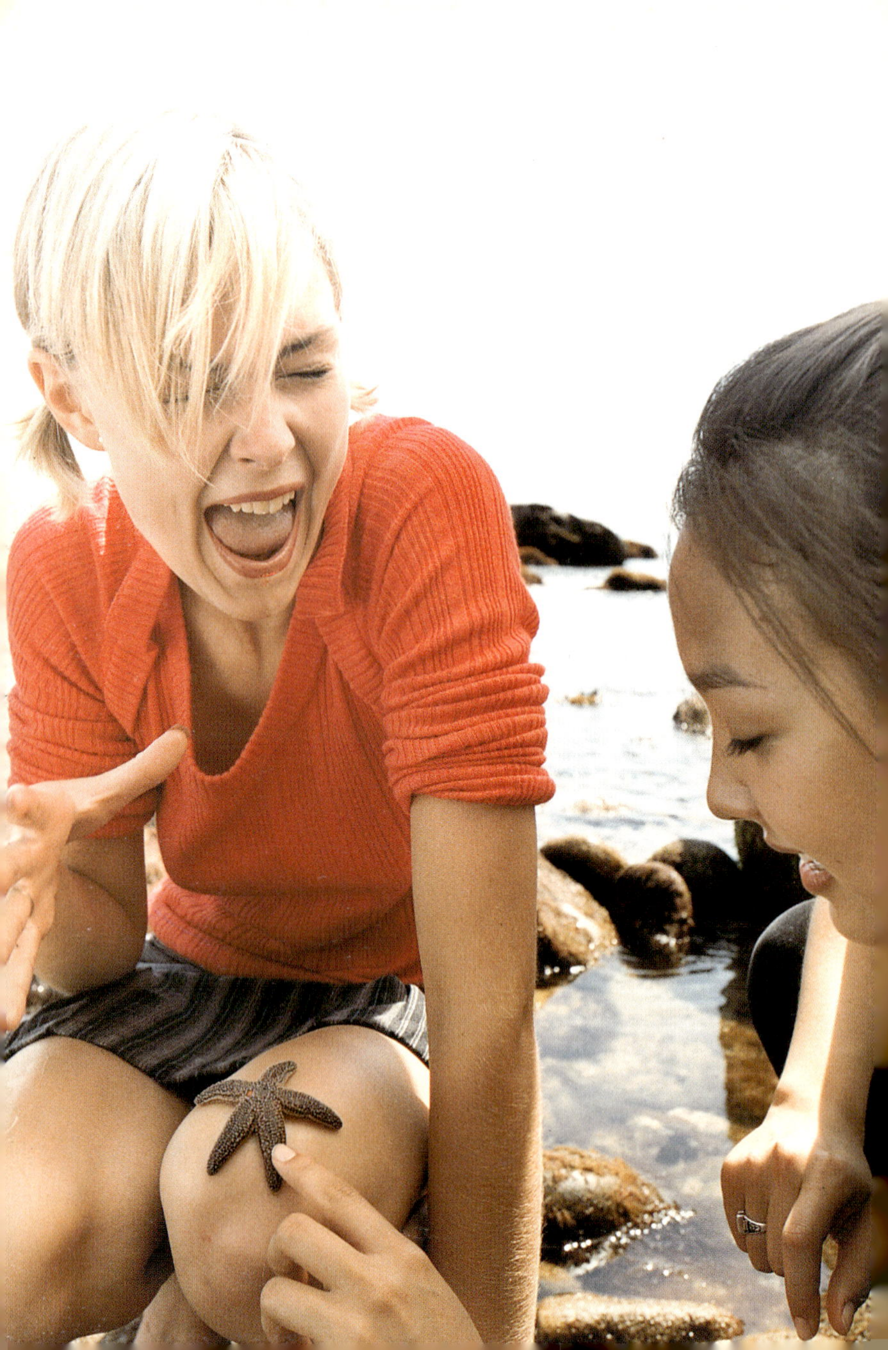

5. **When your boss catches you showing up 15 minutes late for work, you:**
a. Apologize and make up a white lie about hitting unexpected traffic.
b. Mumble, "Sorry," then complain to coworkers that she's a tyrant.
c. Make up some kooky story about helping a friend with an emergency.
d. Look her in the eye, apologize, and tell her it won't happen again.

6. **Your parents are trusting you to stay home alone this weekend while they're at a wedding. You:**
a. Send out an Evite for everyone to stop by Saturday night.
b. Invite a small group of friends over to hang out.
c. Use the extra quiet time to work on all those college essays.
d. Wear pajamas all weekend and watch movies on Lifetime.

Do some quick math to see whether you act your age...or your shoe size.

6-9 points:

babe in toyland

You still have that totally carefree attitude you had in grade school. Sometimes you don't consider the effects of your actions; start weighing pros and cons before just jumping into big decisions.

ANSWER KEY:
1: a = 3, b = 2, c = 1, d = 4;
2: a = 1, b = 4, c = 2, d = 3;
3: a = 1, b = 2; c = 3, d = 4;
4: a = 4, b = 3, c = 2, d = 1;
5: a = 3, b = 1, c = 2, d = 4;
6: a = 1, b = 2, c = 4, d = 3

10-14 points:

kid at heart

You're free-spirited—and refreshing to be around! But adults may be wary of giving you too much freedom because you seem distracted. Prove your reliability by following through more often.

15-19 points:

teen (in) spirit

You have fun without being reckless and can see others' perspectives, which is why people are drawn to you. Just make sure you continue to balance responsibility with having a good time.

20-24 points:

woman at work

You're responsible and always do the "right" thing. But make sure that you can recognize good risks from bad ones. That way you won't be held back in life for fear of "messing up."

WHAT KIND OF DAUGHTER ARE YOU?

Do your neighbors wish you were theirs? Or do they count their blessings that you're not?

1. Your curfew is:
a. Not an issue—I'm home by then anyway.
b. Not negotiable.
c. More of an ETA, since I'm sometimes late.
d. A joke.

2. What's the main reason to get A's?
a. So I don't get in trouble.
b. So I can get into college.
c. Because I feel good about myself when I do well.
d. There is no reason.

3. The summer job you'd want is:
a. Babysitting.
b. Working at the mall.
c. Volunteering at an animal shelter.
d. Roadie for a rock group.

4. Do you ever clean around the house?
a. Of course, we all help.
b. Yes, I have chores.
c. When it gets messy.
d. Yeah—I clean out the cabinets by snacking!

5. Which character do you identify with?
a. Sweet Lucy on *7th Heaven*.
b. Thoughtful *Felicity*.
c. Fun Phoebe on *Charmed*.
d. Rebel Jen on *Dawson's*.

6. Could you go far away for college?
a. No way! Too scary.
b. Yes, if that's where the best school is.
c. Sure, I'd like to.
d. Could I? I can't wait to!

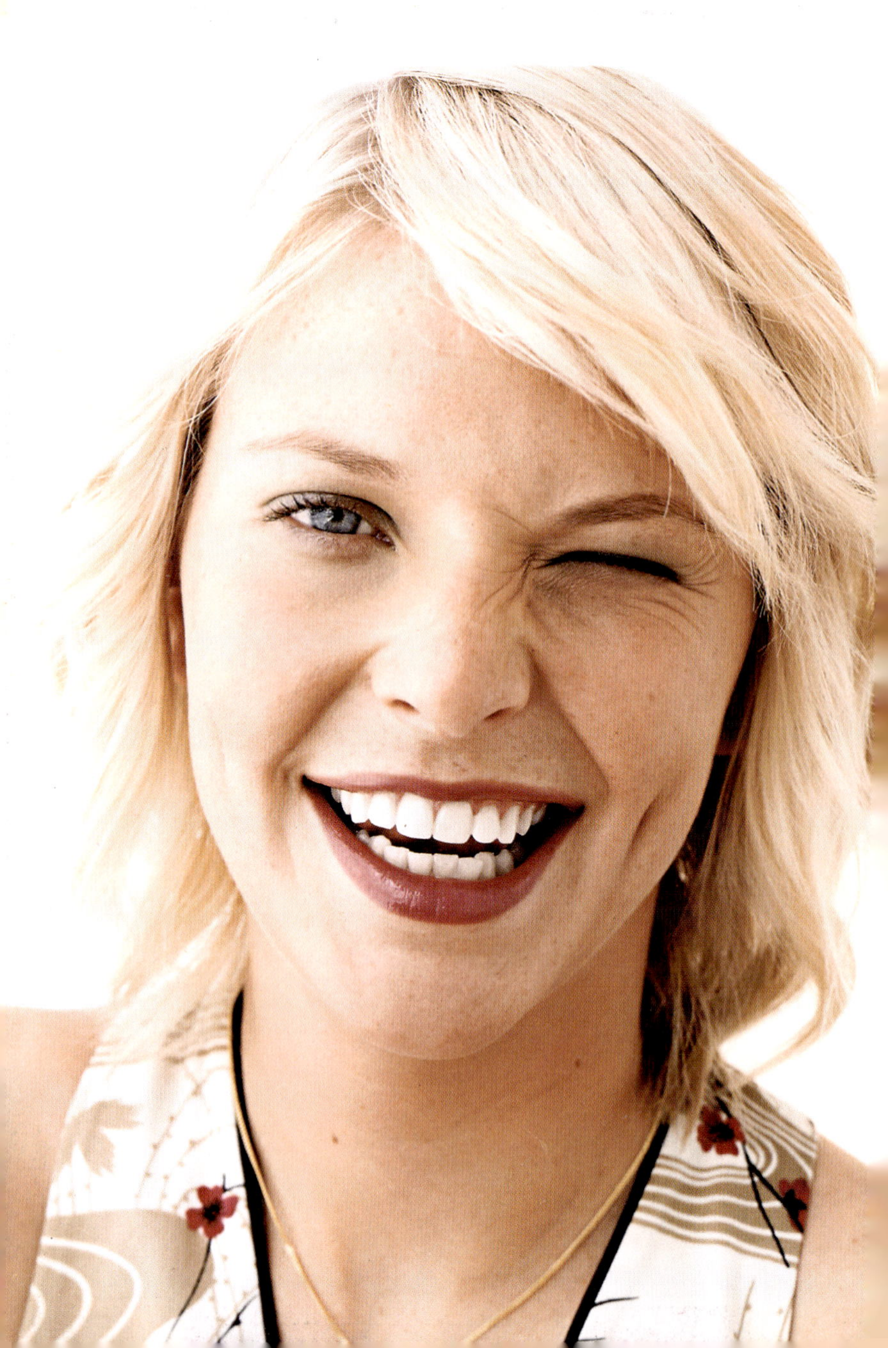

6-10 points:

Mama & Daddy's Little Girl Your parents are as much a part of your decisions as your friends. You can talk to them about almost anything. But don't worry about pushing the rules a little—that's part of growing up, and your parents will love your independent side too.

11-15 points:

First Daughter You're responsible, trustworthy, and you make Mom and Dad proud. As long as you're trying hard because you want to (not just to please the folks), you'll be successful at all you do. Even when you do something wild, your parents still know you respect them (because you actually ask before you dye your hair blue!).

16-19 points:

Independent Offspring You have a good relationship with your parents—you know they'll always be behind you. Since they trust you, they're happy to let you go for your goals, even if it means you might move far away.

20-24 points:

Wild Child You want to live your life your way—and who can blame you? But next time you feel penned in by parental rules, think about why they exist (to keep you safe!). Show them that you have good judgment—they'll trust you and be more likely to extend that curfew!

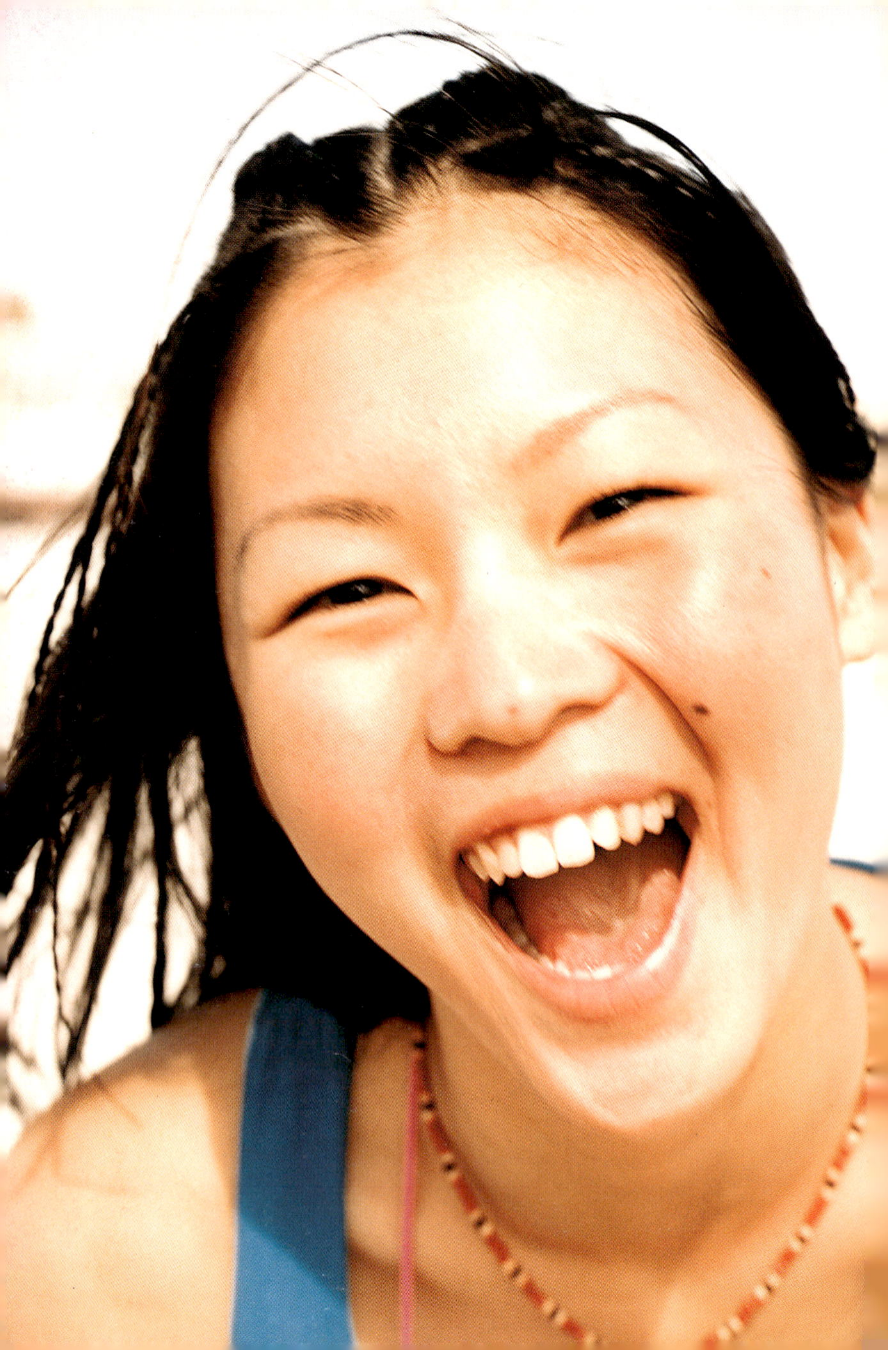

HOW DO GUYS SEE YOU?

Your mom thinks you're beautiful. Your friends say you're the best. But what is that guy thinking?

1. **You're at a Friday-night party relaxing on the couch with friends when (yes—just as you'd hoped) your crush walks in. What do you do?**
a. Find a way to ditch your friends (they'll understand, right?), and go over and talk to him before some other girl corners him.
b. Catch his eye, smile and wave, and then go right back to talking to your friends (for now, anyway).
c. Avoid eye contact while sending him mental "I like you" vibes.

2. **Same party. So, who is it you're hanging out with on that couch mentioned in the first question?**
a. Either all of your girlfriends or a bunch of guy friends.
b. Some girls, some guys.
c. Your best friend, you're having an intense one-on-one discussion.

3. **Okay, we promise this will be the last party question: What, most likely, are you wearing?**
a. Short skirt, tight top—it's a party!
b. Your sexiest jeans, a cute party top, and maybe a little extra lip stuff.
c. Probably the same thing you wore to school that day.

4. **If you had to sum up your entire life's relationship history with guys, you'd say you've had:**
a. A few summer flings, at least three boyfriends since the beginning of high school, and your fair share of hookups on weekends.
b. Lots of guy friends, zero to three boyfriends, and maybe one or two (max!) hookups (or none at all).
c. One really serious long-term boyfriend or crush, and not very many guy friends.

5. So there you are, sitting in calc class directly behind your crush, when you notice that (ay, ay, ay!) his tag is sticking out of the back of his shirt. What do you do?
a. Relish the opportunity to fix it and let your fingers oh so casually linger on his gorgeous neck for a couple of seconds longer.
b. Whisper, "Hey, your tag's sticking out," and then quickly tuck it in with a cute little pat.
c. Just do nothing—even if you do (go ahead, admit it!) daydream about massaging his neck.

6. How would you describe your friends (i.e., the people he sees you with every day)?
a. A big but tight circle. You eat lunch, study, and party together.
b. A few different groups: your best friends, your teammates, and of course, your HBO-addict friends.
c. An extremely close small group.

7. Be honest: When it comes to guys, do you think it's accurate to say that you have a "type"?
a. Yes! All the guys you've liked tend to fit into the same physical mold.
b. Sure, but in more of a personality way than a physical one.
c. Not really. Every guy you've liked is totally different from the last.

Scoring

Give yourself 3 points for every a, 2 for every b, and 1 for every c. Now add 'em up.

17-21 points: **Intimidating**

You're outgoing, fun, and popular. But . . . the guys who are gutsy enough to approach you can be cockier than a rooster on Viagra (scary!). And nicer guys are afraid you'll reject them. To make them relax, try a new activity so they'll see that you like being with people other than your usual crowd. Also, turn down your flirting a notch. Just waving to him at a party can give him the confidence to come up to *you*.

12-16 points: **Sweet**

You've got self-confidence, and guys flock to that like mice to cheese fondue. By hanging out with people in different crowds, looking your best but not overdoing it, and being a mix of friendly and flirty, you show guys you're interested in them as people. P.S. If you're into a guy friend, be a *little* flirtier so he knows you're *not* just one of the guys.

7-11 points: **Mysterious**

You're private, so guys who like you can't tell enough *about* you to know what to say. If you like him, help him! Mention something you have in common: "I hear you like fly-fishing. My dad and I just went." Don't know him well? Bring up a current event. Hey, even a *smile* can show him you'd like to talk.

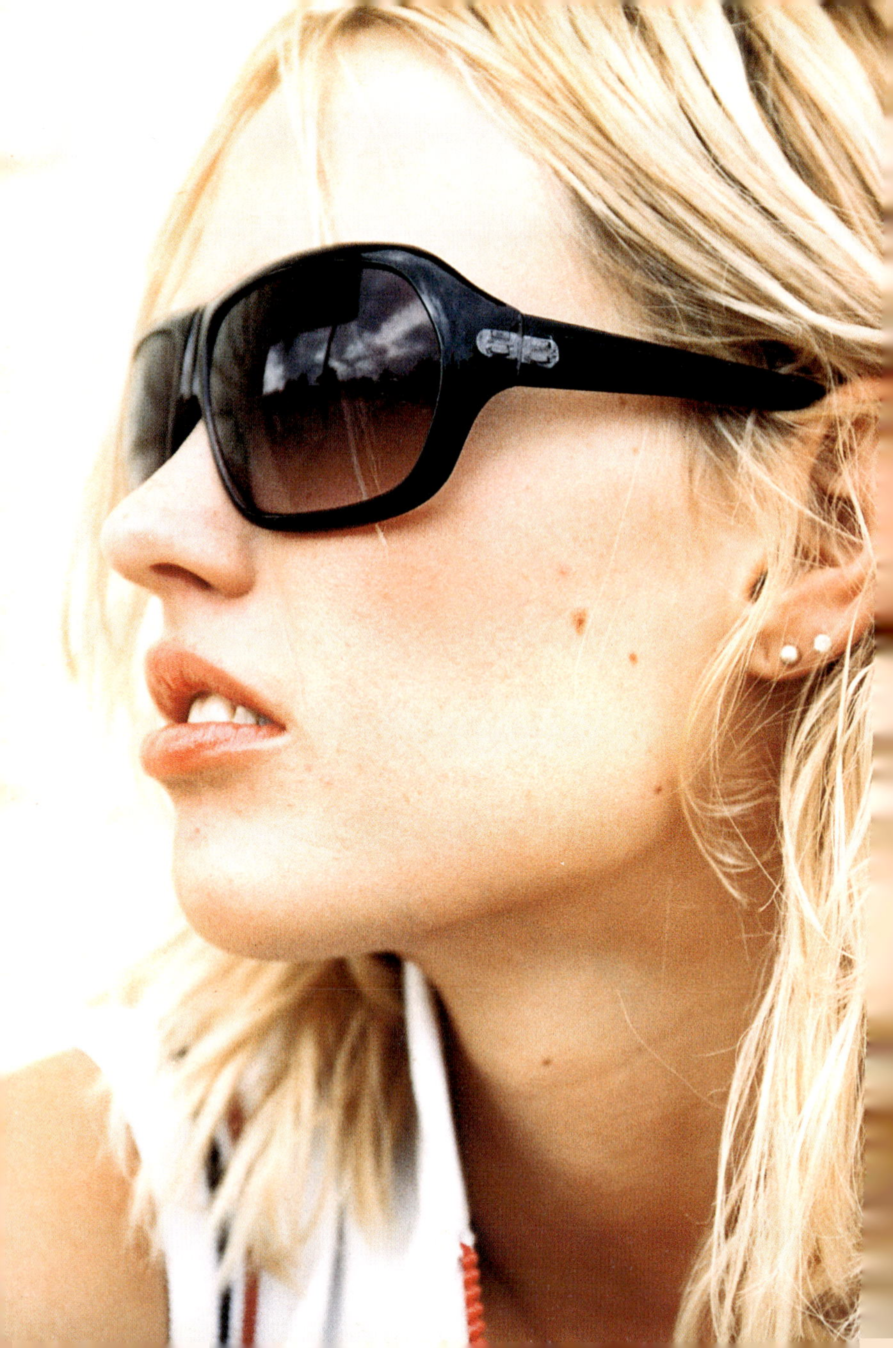

ATTITUDE CHECK!

Do you roll with the punches or spark up drama?

1. Your family vacation to the Bahamas is canceled because of the hurricane. You...

a. Roll your eyes and mutter "This really sucks" loud enough for your parents to hear, then slam your bedroom door.
b. Freak out. Your entire spring break is ruined because you'll be the only one to go back to school without a tan.
c. Shrug it off. At least you found out about the storm before you spent your entire allowance on a new bikini. Phew!

2. You drop a huge tray of glasses while waiting on tables. You...

a. Tell your boss it was the stupid busboy's fault for leaving the floor wet.
b. Turn bright red and start to cry.
c. Bow and thank the customers for their applause, then promise your manager you'll be more careful in the future.

3. Your father's company is relocating your family from sunny California to a tiny ski town thousands of miles away. You...

a. Tell your parents they're crazy if they think you're moving to Nowheresville. Military school sounds like more fun.
b. Kiss your social life goodbye. These are supposed to be the best years of your life, but now they'll be the worst!
c. Can't wait to check out the cute guys on the slopes. Look out!

4. Your friend is throwing a huge April Fools' Day costume party and you need a getup. You...

a. Boycott the bash. Dressing up in ridiculous costumes is so not your idea of a good time.
b. Spend hours on the night of the party frantically hunting around in your mom's closet for something—anything—to wear.

c. Get in the spirit by dressing up as a zombie cheerleader.

5. Your best bud starts dating a cute guy from another school. When she tells you about their super-romantic date, you think:

a. "Could she be sappier? All this lovey-dovey stuff is making me nauseous."
b. "She's so perfect—all she has to do is look at a guy and he's fully in love with her. I'll never have a boyfriend."
c. "How amazing for her! I can't wait until someone takes me on a date like that!"

6. The first college you get a response from turns you down. Your immediate reaction is:

a. "How could they reject me? That loser from down the block got in last year..."
b. "I'm a total failure. I'll probably end up living with my parents forever."
c. "Oh shoot! It's a good thing I applied to a bunch of different schools."

7. Your math teacher springs a pop quiz on you and you know you bombed it. You...

a. Complain to your mom that your teacher is way too harsh—and has it in for you.
b. Throw a fit after class and tell your teacher she must let you take it again. This time you promise you'll do well!
c. Plan on doing extra credit. There's got to be a way you can save your grade.

Scoring

Give yourself 1 point for every a, 2 points for every b, and 3 points for every c.

17 to 21 points: **Super-positive Girl**

Even when you're majorly embarrassed or really disappointed, you focus on finding a solution, not wallowing in the problem. But sometimes you stifle *your* feelings just to keep everyone else happy. If something bad happens, spill your guts to a trusted pal. Expressing your emotions will make you feel better—plus, you'll get to bond with your bud.

12 to 16 points: **The Drama Queen**

You make a big deal out of *everything*. But constantly freaking out is exhausting. To help figure out what is—and what's not—worth your energy, start keeping a journal. Every time catastrophe strikes, write it down and at the end of a month, reread your entries. You'll realize that only one (okay, maybe two) of your freak-outs was truly legit. The rest were minor glitches that now seem silly. Soon you'll be solving probs with solutions instead of stressful sob sessions.

7 to 11 points: **Miss Cranky-Pants**

You're never afraid to say what you think—but, you usually think everything sucks. When you're always looking for the downside, you don't open yourself up to anything good that might happen. To tune up your 'tude, try this: Every time you say something nasty, put a dollar in a jar. As the money piles up, you'll realize how often you're not so nice. Then use the cash to do something sweet for the people you've been mean to.

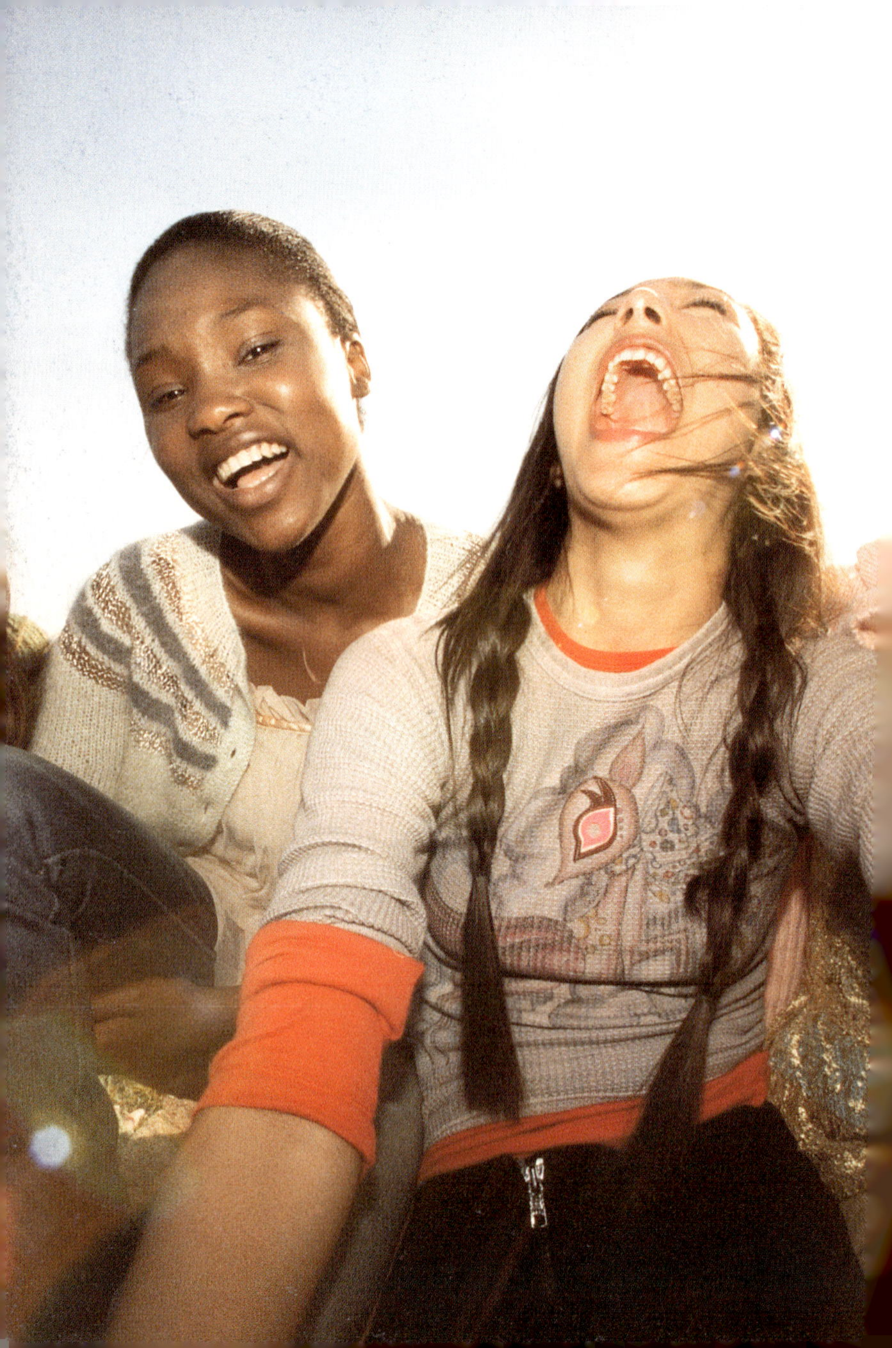

Circle of Friends

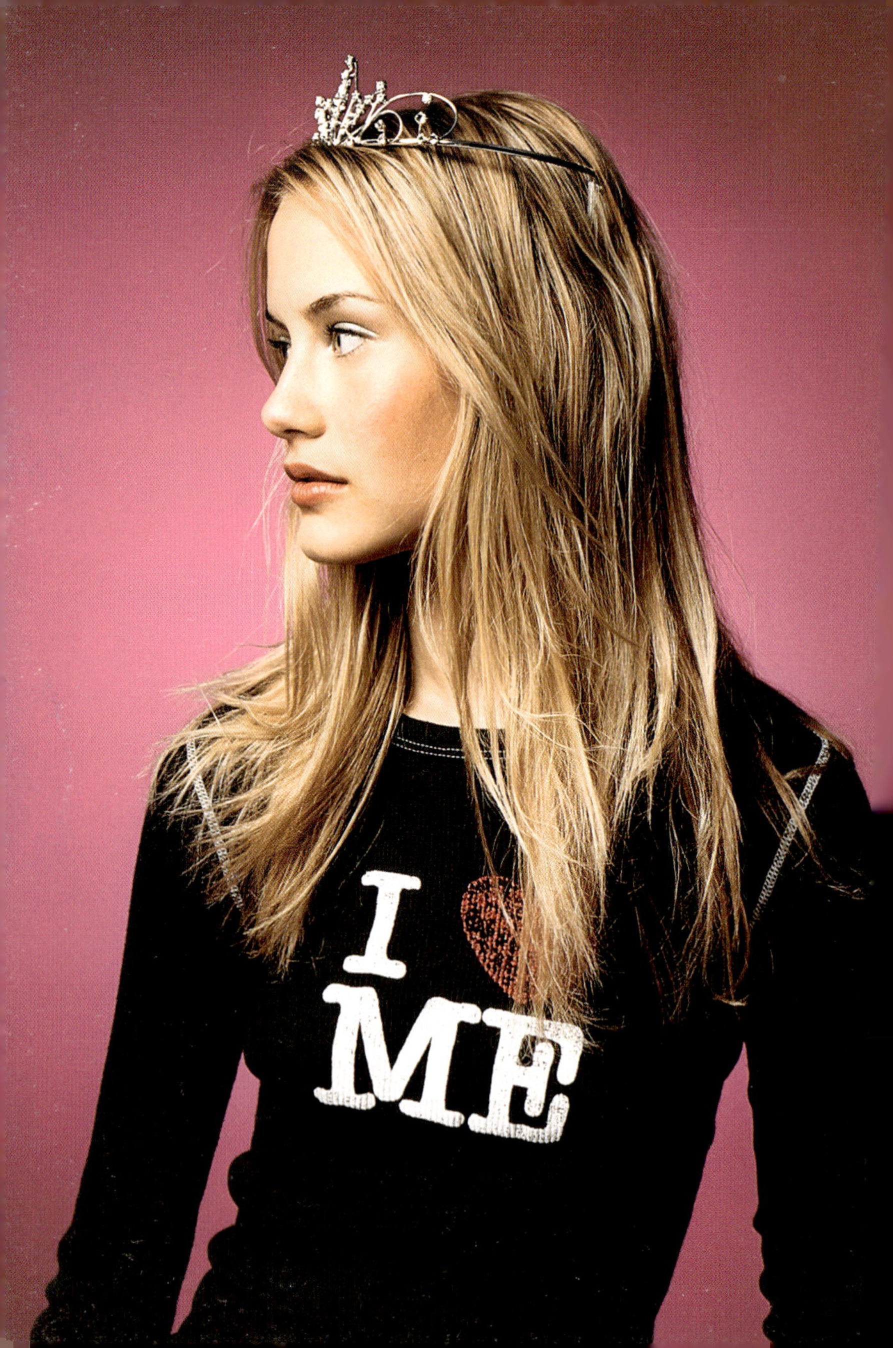
I ME

WHAT DO PEOPLE THINK OF YOU?

You're not paranoid for wanting to know. You're human.

This quiz is designed to show you how other people see you and what you can do if that's not who you really are inside. Answer these Qs according to what you'd actually do, not what you wish you'd do. Then read on to find out if the impression you give truly reflects the inner you. If not, we'll show you how to bring out the side you're hiding, so the world can see your real amazing self!

1. You're cruising in your car with your friends and you accidentally hit the car in front of you. You:
a. Sit there in shock.
b. Flip out and yell at the other driver.
c. Roll your eyes and pull over.
d. Get out and start exchanging your insurance info with the other driver.

2. You're sitting in class, and the teacher asks a question you totally know the answer to. What do you do?
a. Let someone else answer it, in case you're wrong.
b. Just blurt the answer right out.
c. Don't answer—you're too busy drawing in your notebook to bother.
d. Raise your hand.

3. It's 3 p.m. You and your friends are in the school hallway. Your crush is approaching, so you:
a. Quickly turn and talk to your friends so he won't realize you noticed him.
b. Keep talking to your friends, and then bust on his outfit (in a funny way) when he walks by.
c. Stare him down as he passes you to see if you can catch his eye.
d. Wait until he gets near you, smile, and say, "Hi, Jake, what's up?"

4. **A friend calls to tell you about a new guy she likes and goes on and on (and on!) about it. So you:**

a. Let her talk for as long as she wants.
b. Say, "That sounds just like me and _____ (your crush's name)!"
c. Listen for a few minutes before you get bored and start flipping through the TV channels while she talks.
d. Cut to the chase by saying, "So are you going to call him?"

5. **You're clothes shopping, and you need a different size. The salesperson keeps ignoring you to help other customers. You:**

a. Just stand there patiently, hoping she'll look at you sometime soon.
b. Clear your throat loudly and start complaining to your friend.
c. Get annoyed and leave—that shirt was too preppy looking, anyway.
d. Walk over and say, "Excuse me, is there someone who can help me?"

6. **There's a college fair at your school over the weekend, and everyone is "strongly encouraged" to go. You:**

a. Go and walk around quietly collecting brochures. If you have questions, you'll just call later.
b. Grab some stuff in the first five minutes, then start talking to some of the other kids about which colleges have the best party scenes.
c. Don't go—the alternative kinds of schools you'll be applying to probably won't be there anyway.
d. Go, armed with a list of questions to ask the admissions people at all five of your top-choice schools.

7. **Your friend begs you to go to the Fake Brain concert with her, but you're so not into them. You:**

a. Go anyway to be a good friend.
b. Tell her you'll go as long as she'll agree to hang out after the show and get some pizza with your friends.
c. Tell her sorry, you'd rather get a Brazilian bikini wax. (Youch!)
d. Tell her no thanks, but name three people you know would love to go.

Scoring

The letter you chose the most reflects the way people see you. Got a tie between two or even three letters? Ask a friend if she thinks you chose the right answers for you. But it's possible you could be a mix of types—so read each with an open mind and see which one sounds the most like you.

Mostly a's: Miss Introspective. First impression? Quiet and observant, you prefer to let others take the lead. You're seen as a shy girl, but also as a caring, considerate friend—the one everyone comes to when they need a nurturing shoulder to cry on. You're happy to listen to your friends, and you're never pushy with your opinions—instead, you keep them to yourself or write them in a journal. People often tend to wonder what thoughts lie behind your knowing eyes.

Doesn't sound like the REAL you? When you're asked to describe yourself, shy isn't the word you'd use. Just because you're quiet doesn't mean you haven't got some totally wild ideas brewing in your head! So get ready to surprise people with them.

Tip 1: Practice speaking your mind. After you're in a group situation, write down what you were feeling and what (or who) may have stopped you from saying or doing what you wanted. Also write down the things you wanted to say or do but didn't. Knowing exactly what those things are is almost like planning for what you'll do in the future. Next time you're with your friends, wait for those short pauses in the conversation, then jump in with your thoughts or opinions.

Tip 2: When you're in a big group, make sure you stand toward the center of the crowd, instead of off to one side. People will expect to hear more from you, so you'll be forced to let your thoughts loose more often.

Tip 3: Try to take more chances. Go to a café alone or join a club at school that none of your good friends are in. Once you're out of the shadows of your crowd, you'll have to speak up. Soon you'll be more comfortable letting your inner self shine...that is, when you feel like it!

Mostly b's: Social Butterfly. First impression? Outgoing and extroverted, you've got lots of friends in all different groups. People have stereotyped you as a party girl because you're always up for doing something social, and you're the one who always knows the plan for Saturday night. Since you're not afraid to open your mouth to express an opinion or tell someone what you think of them, people feel there's never a dull moment when you're around. Doesn't sound like the REAL you? You know how you always read interviews with celebrities known for lavish partying and they say, "That's so not me—I'm really down-to-earth"? You may be kind of like that—you feel totally laid-back and yet for some reason everyone thinks you're this wild party girl. Here's how to let people see more of your serious side.

Tip 1: As great as you are at it, resist the urge to entertain! Next time you want to give your shocking or sassy opinion, pause and count to three. Is it really worth it? If so, go for it! But look at every opportunity as a chance to give a more thoughtful or heartfelt (instead of just crazy!) opinion instead.

Tip 2: Stand on the edge of the group instead of in the middle, at least some of the time. That makes others take the floor, and you'll get to take a nice break from always being the center of attention.

Tip 3: Once a weekend, hang out with your closest friends doing something low-key. Don't feel you're letting people down by not showing up at a party. Sometimes being offstage can remind you what it feels like to be the real you.

Mostly c's: Independent Woman. First impression? Some people who don't know you might think you're a little standoffish, since you don't usually make the first move to talk to them. You're known around school as the girl who doesn't seem to care what anyone else thinks and doesn't feel the need to belong. Since you go your own way in what you wear, the music you listen to, and most other things, too, people think you're totally over all the stuff they're still insecure about.

Doesn't sound like the REAL you? Sometimes the people who seem totally "cool" and alternative on the outside are as cuddly as teddy bears on the inside. (Like, Marilyn Manson's not scary when you hear him in an interview, right?) You can make yourself just a little more approachable too, if that's what you want.

Tip 1: Use your passions to connect with people. If you're an environmentalist, organize a peaceful protest against deforestation; if you design jewelry, start selling it. This way, you'll interact with people, and they'll see the real girl behind your cool, mysterious facade.

Tip 2: You might think school clubs are so not you, but if you get involved in one that you can get into—like photography or drama—you might be surprised to find out that even kids who look the most "mainstream" on the outside are nice and weird (in a good way—the way we all are!) once you know them.

Tip 3: Try not to separate yourself from the crowd just to prove you won't conform. If you get the urge to go to a school dance and boogie to BSB songs, don't not do it because it doesn't go along with your image. Seeing you at a dance is the last thing anyone would expect of you, so you're still being your rebellious self. Ha!

Mostly d's: Organizational Queen. First impression? You are goal-oriented and driven—the girl who people see as totally mature beyond high school. You're the one your friends come to when they've got a problem that needs solving—fast. They respect you for being so put together (okay, and they're jealous of your college résumé), but sometimes they wish you'd make more time to just kick back and relax.

Doesn't sound like the REAL you? Maybe you've got this fun-loving person inside who, you'll admit, you haven't let out much lately since school keeps you way too busy. Understandable, but if you'd rather fit more of your fun self into your college-bound schedule, here's what you can do.

Tip 1: Take lessons with a friend in something noncompetitive—like pottery or baking. Don't worry about being the best at it—in fact, choose a hobby that you may kind of suck at. (C'mon, you can find something!) The point is to just have fun.

Tip 2: Since you're a great organizer, plan one activity a month for you and your friends where there's no purpose other than to make fools of yourselves and laugh your butts off (karaoke or bowling would be perfect!).

Tip 3: Show your friends that you can direct your energy toward being a friend just as well as you can put it toward acing an exam. If you really are busy when a friend calls, tell her you'll call her at a certain time later, and when it's that time, put aside what you're doing and give her your full attention. Hey, it'll give you a break and help her out at the same time. How's that for being efficient?

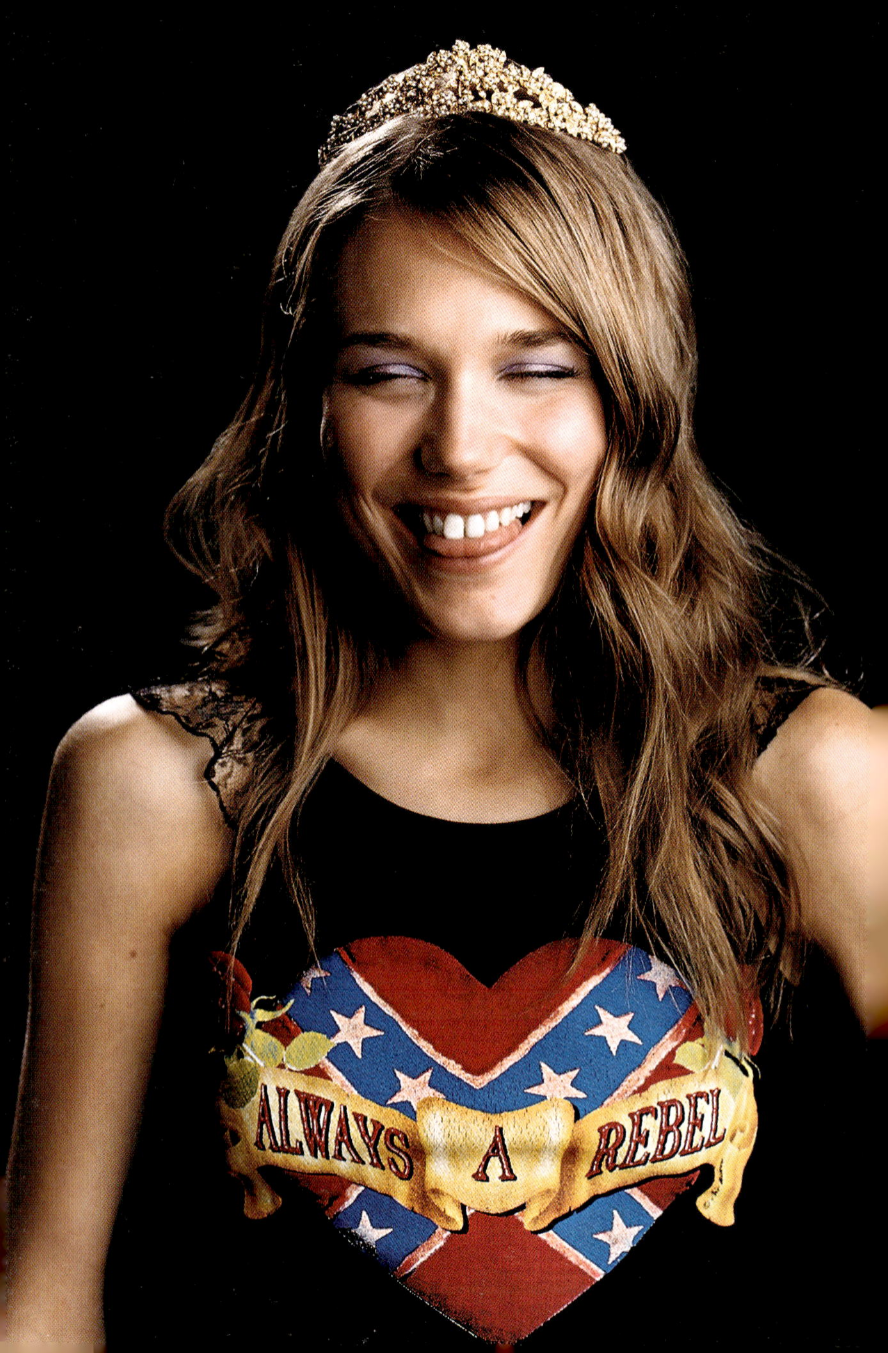
ALWAYS A REBEL

FIND YOUR INNER PARTY ANIMAL

Figure out your social prowess and work it!

1. If you planned an end-of-school event, it would be:
a. A "school's out" film fest: *Summer School, Dazed and Confused, Heathers,* etc.
b. Trading yearbooks at a fun restaurant.
c. A tiki-theme beach party.

2. If you're not dancing at a school function, it's because...
a. I'm waiting for someone to physically force me to.
b. I'm just waiting till the party really gets going.
c. I'm too busy talking with my friends.

3. Have you ever made out at a party?
a. No way—I think that's really tacky.
b. Yeah, but only playing party games and stuff.
c. Um, yeah. Hasn't everyone?

4. At a good club, there are always lots of:
a. Cushy couches to hang out on.
b. Square feet, so me and my friends can claim our own space.
c. People, even after it gets late.

5. At a friend's b-day bash, you spend the most time:
a. Getting to know one of her other friends better.
b. Catching up with my five best friends.
c. Running around, trying to find time to say hi to everyone.

6. It's a Friday night fiesta. What are you wearing?
a. Whatever I had on at school that day.
b. A comfortable (but really pretty!) outfit.
c. My amazing tube top and skirt—where else can I wear them?!

Add 'em up! Give yourself 1 point for each a, 2 for each b, and 3 for each c.

6-9 points: Lone Wolf
At big events, you show up, say hi, and split when your ears start ringing. But that doesn't mean you're not social—hello! You'd just rather pair off for one-on-one hangouts. If you do find yourself stuck at a huge party, just get comfortable by chatting with a few select people.

10-14 points: Laid-Back Lion
You travel in a pack at parties, so you always have fun (whether the soirée is cool or not). You also know your own moods—if you don't want to go out, you won't show up and be miserable, you'll just rent videos with friends. Take a turn organizing big stuff too—reserve a table at a pizza place for a low-effort chance at party-planning.

15-18 points: Social Butterfly
Every time you talk to someone at a party, they think to themselves, "I should hang out with her more!" You're an expert matchmaker, and you always make everyone in a group feel welcome. Make it a goal to spend time individually with the people you meet too.

ARE YOU A BORE?

If you were a bagel, would you be plain or everything? Hmm...

1. Midnight. Sleepover party. Truth or Dare. You pick:
a. Dare.
b. Truth.
c. Neither, you totally hate that game.

2. A motivational speaker who's trying to teach your school an "important lesson" whips out a bungee cord, asks for volunteers, and looks right at you. You:
a. Jump out of your seat and head right to the front of the auditorium.
b. Laugh nervously. If she picks you, you'll have to suck it up and go up.
c. Hide behind the big-headed kid sitting in the row in front of you.

3. At a party, you talk to a cutie all night. You two don't make out, but you do seem to have chemistry. (Go, you!) Afterward, when your friends grill you for details, you:
a. Tell them every little detail of his life, including his latest chem grade and what he had for lunch that day.
b. Give them just the juiciest highlights of your conversation.
c. Shrug and say, "I dunno, he's cool."

4. How often do you change the way your bedroom looks (by putting up new posters, moving furniture around, etc.)?
a. At least a couple of times a year. You're always up for a new look.
b. Maybe once a year or so, when you're feeling particularly inspired.
c. Every few years. The last time was back when the Macarena was cool.

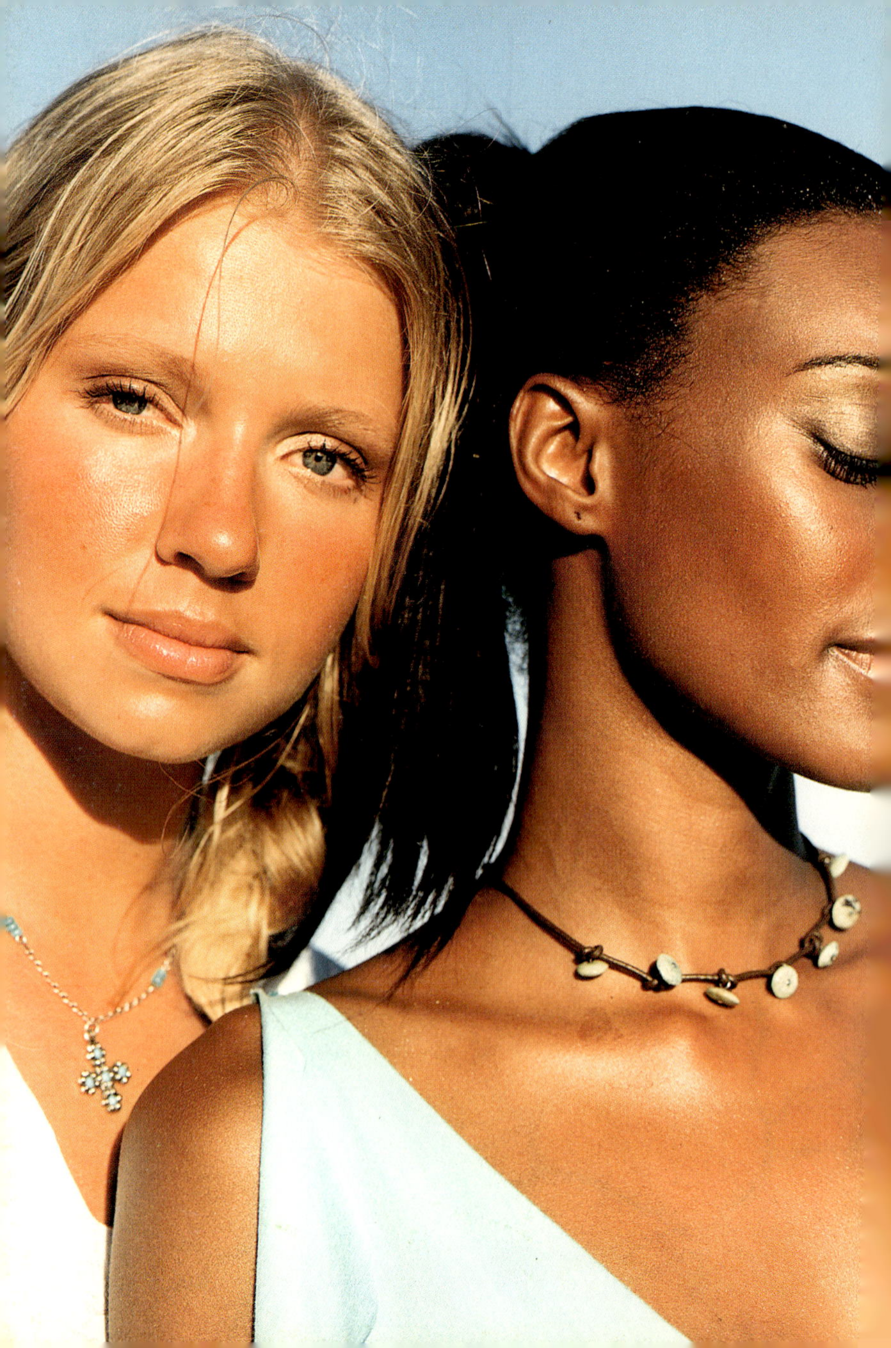

5. Think fast. How many after-school activities are you signed up for?

a. More than 3.
b. 1–3.
c. 0.

6. Let's just say you're having dinner at a friend's house, and her parents serve something you've never had (or even seen) before. What do you do?

a. Try it! (You never know—maybe you'll even ask for seconds.)
b. Try it (but only to be polite).
c. Take some, but shove it around your plate and hope nobody notices.

7. Crunch time! You've got one week to get ready for a big oral report on mountain climbing (a topic you know practically nothing about). You:

a. Take a climbing class and write about your first-person experience.
b. Do research and check out the local gear shop to talk to some expert climbers about their adventures.
c. Read some stuff on the Internet and write up the how-to.

Scoring

Mostly a's

Wild Woman

You couldn't be boring if you tried. Sailing? Why not? Cool new club? Sure! Driving a convertible in the snow? Um, yeah. Well...sometimes your sense of adventure can get the best of you. So, if you're about to try something wild, stop and ask yourself if you really want to do it for you—not just to impress other people.

Dare: The next time a friend of yours is sad, use your wild instincts to cheer her up. Pick out crazy vintage clothes together at a thrift store and wear them out dancing that night!

Mostly b's

Fun Compadre

You're adventurous enough to try to get backstage after an awesome concert or perfectly happy just listening to CDs with a friend. You're confidently spontaneous, willing to be wild one day and tame the next, and that makes people like you. They know the real you, and you get the amazing feeling of knowing they like you just as you are.

Dare: List the three most "boring" things in your life (like Saturday SAT class or babysitting for the Blues Clues–addicted Johnson twins, again), then figure out a way to make them exciting—like asking Mrs. Johnson if you can take her darling girls to the movies!

Mostly c's

Miss Consistent

You're kind, loyal, and rock steady, and people love you for it. But if you change your routine, you'll have more fun. Sure, always ordering chicken parm is fine now, but eventually you will get sick of it. And (not to freak you out) if you always hang out with the same crowd, what if you get sick of them? So shake things up! Be bold! Order eggplant parmigiana and go to a par-tay this weekend.

Dare: Any time you're about to do something automatically, change it just a wee bit. You never know when a "happy accident" (like meeting a new guy at the Coke machine—not the Pepsi machine) could rock your world!

WHAT KIND OF FRIEND ARE YOU?

Reveal the reasons why your best pals think you're so great!

_____ It seems like your best friend and her boyfriend are always fighting. Their latest spat was five minutes ago. Give yourself one point if you're already on your way to her house with a box of Kleenex and pint of B&J; two points if you're on the phone with her telling her to lose the loser already; three points if you tell her you're on the other line, but you'll call her back in two minutes.

_____ It's Friday night and you're cruising around with your usual crowd. Add one point if you're going to be the group's chauffeur (again!); two points if you agree to drive—if everyone chips in for gas; three points if you secretly love to drive because that means you can hit every party you want!

_____ Your friend is on the verge of failing French. Add one point if you put aside your own studying to be her personal tutor; two points if you suggest she drop a few of her many extracurricular activities and make time to hit the books; three points if you round up a bunch of friends to take her to Rock 'n' Bowl and get her mind off it.

_____ You and your best friend were invited to what's already being called the Party of the Year. The problem? Her heinous ex is going too. Give yourself one point if you pass on the party and go to a movie with your friend instead; two points if you try to get the party's host to disinvite the ex; three points if you convince your B.F. to put on a happy face—and a hot outfit—and party hearty.

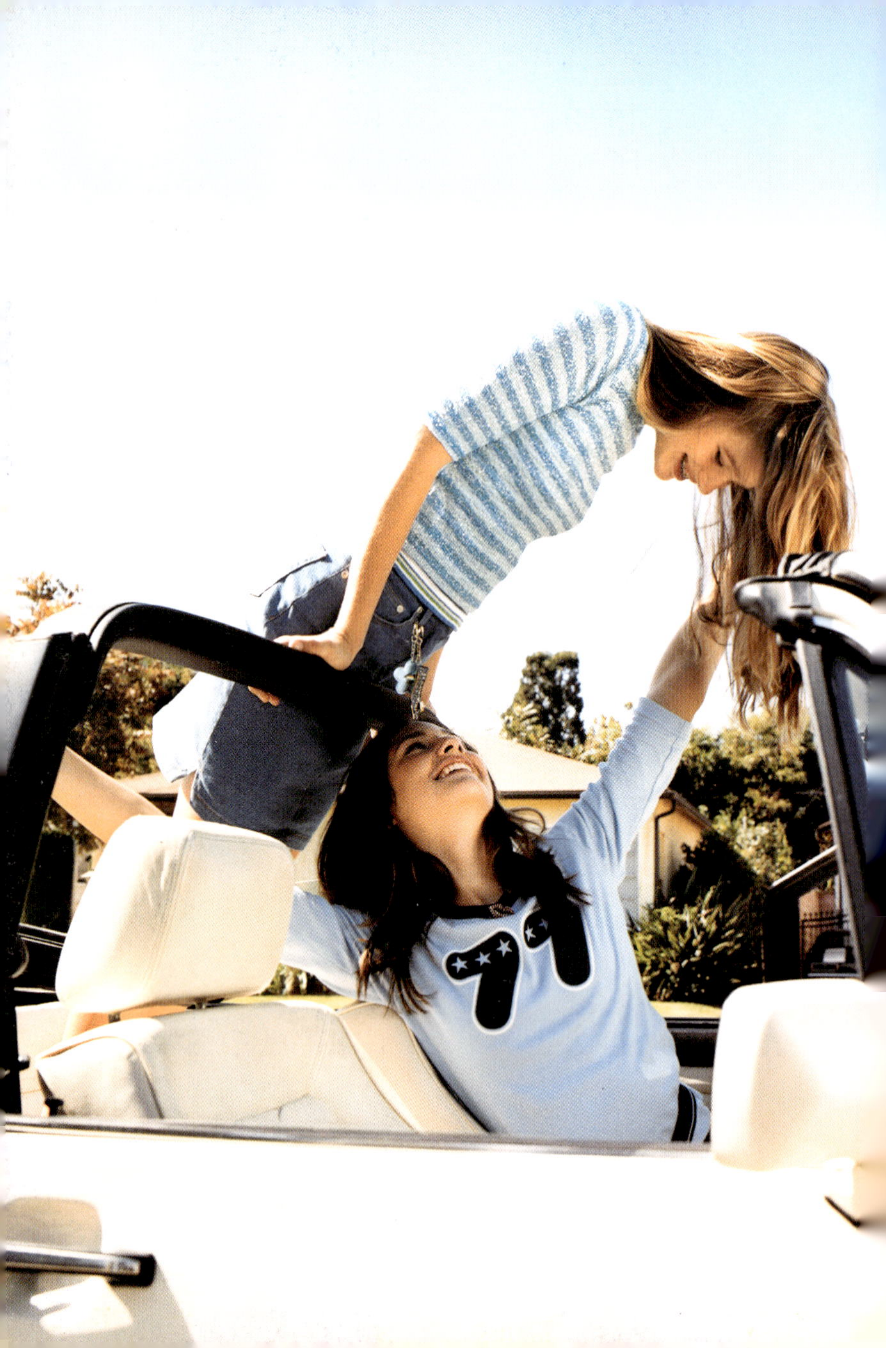

_____ It's your birthday and your Gram stuffed your card with cash. Now you can: lend [insert broke friend's name here] that money she needs (add one point); buy yourself that MAC lipstick you've been eyeing (add two points); go with all your friends to see 'N Sync in concert (add three points).

_____ You hear the phone ring, and your mom says, "It's for you..." Chances are: someone in one of your classes wants to borrow your notes (add one point); a girlfriend needs your immediate attention to help decode her crush's recent strange behavior (add two points); a conference call awaits—two of your best buds want to know what's up for the weekend (add three points).

_____ You'd planned a mellow night at home when your friend calls and asks you to take over her babysitting gig so she can go out with her crush. Add one point if you happily volunteer—hey, at least you'll make a little extra cash; two points if you agree to fill in—after suggesting she return the favor by lending you her new black dress for the next big party; three points if you say "Okay—but only if I can invite some people to come over and hang."

_____ A friend asks to borrow $10, clearly forgetting she owes you $20 from last month. Add one point if you fork over the dough and figure you'll remind her later; two points if you say "Hello, I don't have 10 bucks—I lent you 20 last month, and you still haven't paid me back"; three points if you give it to her, but only after finding out that she needs it so she can go to the movies with you.

_____ You get a mass e-mail inviting you to a friend's party on Saturday night—tons of cool people will be there. The first thing you think is: "Wonder if they'll need any help setting up" (add one point); "Wonder if they know I really don't like huge parties" (add two points); "Wonder if they'll let me bring my crew too" (add three points).

77

SCORING

22 to 27 points: THE SOCIAL DIRECTOR

Fun is your middle name. You're the plan maker of the pack—and you wouldn't have it any other way! But if you don't remember to carve some solo space on your social calendar, you might get burned out. Don't ever stop having good times; just be sure to hang out alone every once in a while so you can relax and refuel.

15 to 21 points: THE STRAIGHT SHOOTER

You're the ultimate go-to girl for thoughtful advice and truly honest opinions. Keep in mind, though, that while honesty is almost always the best policy, there's a fine line between just right and too harsh. The next time you're tempted to meddle in someone's business (or offer an opinion that wasn't asked for), stop and think about how you would feel if the tables were turned. If the answer is "not great," keep your advice to yourself.

9 to 14 points: THE GIVER

You're always just a phone call away when a friend needs help. Naturally, your gentleness and generosity make you majorly in demand as a best friend. Just don't become a doormat for friends with problems—sometimes you need to ask for help solving your probs too.

ARE YOU ANNOYING?

Find out what people really think of you.

1. The last time a friend confided in you about a problem and asked for your advice, you:
a. Told her what you thought she wanted to hear.
b. Got all the details, gave it some thought, then tried to offer a few helpful suggestions.
c. Listened, then told her about how the same thing had happened to you.

2. On the first day of class your teacher asks you to play the "get to know your neighbor" game. You:
a. Let her go first—you don't want her to think you're self-centered.
b. Ask her a few questions, then share some stuff about yourself.
c. Tell her *everything*—who you're dating, where you were born, what your favorite color is—and before you know it, the bell rings.

3. Which one of the following TV teens would most people compare you with?
a. Willow (on *Buffy the Vampire Slayer*)—she gets along with everybody.
b. Elena (on *Felicity*)—she's got her own stuff to deal with, but she's still there when a friend needs help.
c. Nicole (on *Popular*)—she's not shy about letting everyone know exactly what she wants.

4. You're hanging out at your friends' house after school listening to some BSB. When you get hungry, you:
a. Wait until you get home to eat. You don't want to bother her parents by asking for a snack.
b. Tell your friend you're hungry and then eat whatever she offers.
c. Head straight for the kitchen and raid her fridge.

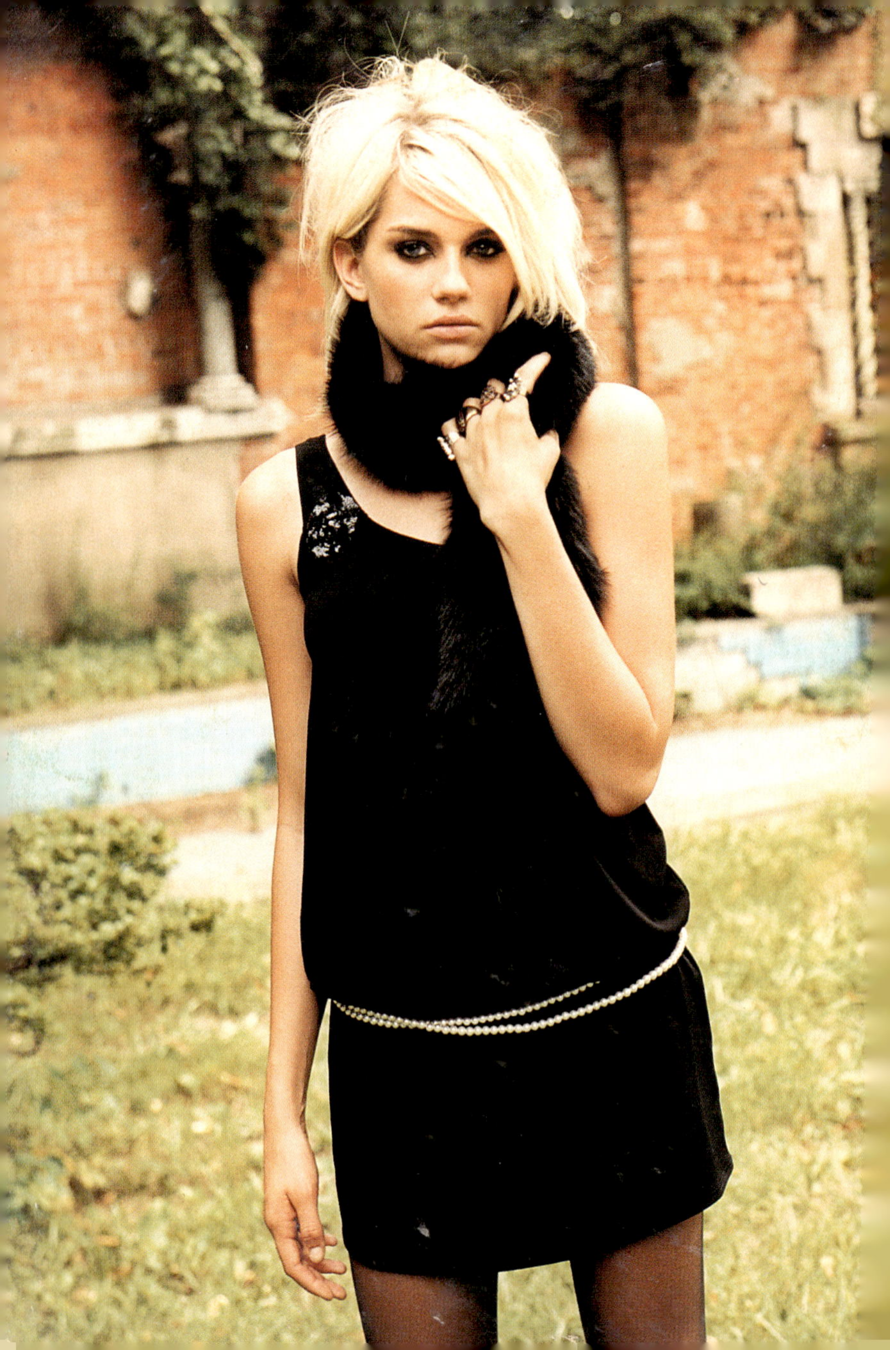

5. **You like your friend's ex, and you feel like this is more than a crush—this *could* be the real thing. You:**
a. Do nothing. A friend's ex is *totally* off-limits no matter what.
b. Talk to your friends about it before making a move.
c. Go for it! Hey, all's fair in love and war.

6. **Your best friend gets a radical new haircut. When she asks you to give her your honest opinion of her new look, you**
a. Tell her you love it—after all, she can't change it *now*.
b. Try to figure out what she's feeling first—if she loves it, great; if not, reassure her that it'll grow out fast.
c. Love it so much you race to that salon to get yours done exactly the same!

7. **When you and your friends head out in a group, how do you decide where you'll go and what you'll do?**
a. You're fine with doing whatever everybody else wants.
b. It's tough making a plan, but you always seem to manage to get everyone to agree on something.
c. You usually try to convince your gang to go to any place where you think you might run into your crush.

Scoring

Mostly a's: Eager to Please

You're not annoying *enough!* It's nice that you're so tuned in to others' needs and feelings, and that you're so careful not to say anything that could be hurtful to anyone. But there are times when you really should be a bit more assertive with your *own* thoughts and desires. Sure, you want everyone to *like* you (who doesn't?), but you don't want to let people walk all over you. Come on, asking a friend for a drink when you're thirsty isn't exactly making a pest of yourself!

Mostly b's: Gets the Hint

You're not too pushy, but you're no *pushover* either. You pay attention to the signals your friends are giving out without letting them automatically have their way all the time. Friends probably think of you as a peacemaker because you're so good at listening to both sides and finding some way to get everybody to agree. And you also know that sometimes a little white lie is the best way to keep the peace—just be careful not to get carried away with those flattering fibs!

Mostly c's: All About Me!

The good news is, you're not afraid to stand up for yourself and ask for what you really want (*and* you usually get it). Of course you don't *mean* for your assertiveness to be annoying, but sometimes it can make you seem a little too self-absorbed. Even your closest friends might get kind of tired of feeling like they always have to do what *you* want to do. Try tuning in better to the signals your friends are giving out—you may find that going along with *their* plans sometimes is actually a lot of fun!

ARE YOU A SUCKER?

Take this quiz to find out whether you're a born BS detector or the butt of everyone's practical jokes.

1. Are you a decent liar?
a. No, I'm terrible at it.
b. I'm okay. Sometimes I can pull it off.
c. Yes, sometimes I even do it just for fun.

2. Have you ever been the victim of an April Fool's joke?
a. Every year.
b. Sure—but I've always gotten my friends back.
c. I don't fall for them, I plan them.

3. A radio station calls and says you won a car. You say:
a. "Cool! What kind?"
b. "Ummm...okay. How'd that happen?"
c. "Who is this?"

4. When did you stop believing in the tooth fairy?
a. You mean there's no tooth fairy?!
b. Between the ages of 6 and 12 years old.
c. Under 6 years old.

5. How many times have you forwarded a chain e-mail?
a. Tons of times—and where's my money?
b. A few times, but then I realized they're hoaxes.
c. Once—all the way to my "delete" box.

6. A guy doesn't call after he says he will. You think:
a. He must have a girlfriend or else he lost my number.
b. He's too nervous or too busy to call.
c. He never meant to call in the first place.

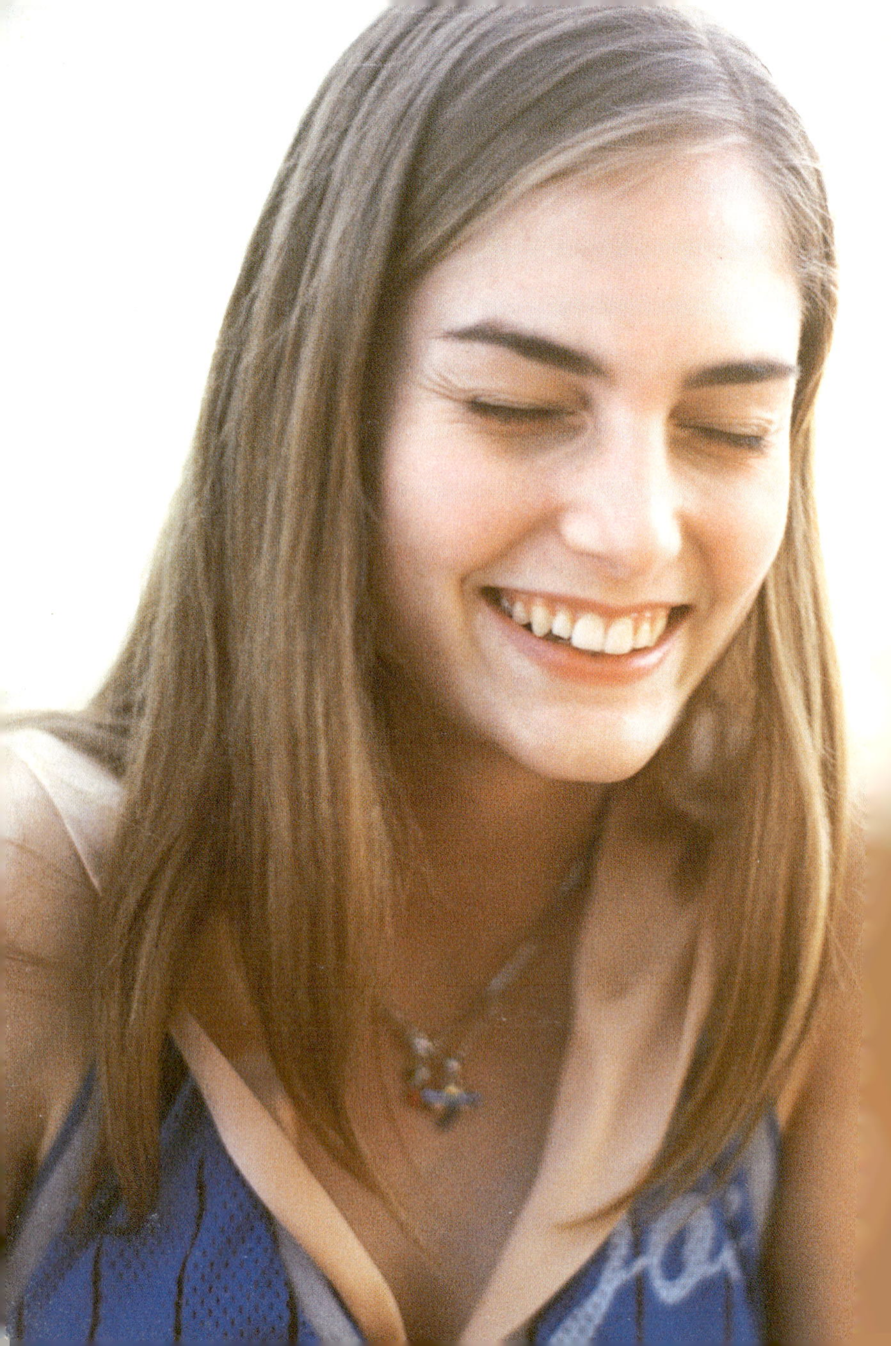

Add 'em up! Give yourself 1 point for each a, 2 for each b, and 3 for each c.

6-9 points: Easily Fooled

You're so trusting that you take everything at face value. That's a nice thing, because it means you always look for the good in everyone. But it could get you in trouble, because people might find that you're a good target for little pranks. You don't have to be the fall guy, though: Just be a little more suspicious when things sound too good to be true—it often means they are.

10-14 points: Radar-Ready Gullible? Not really.

But you're not a cynic, either. You like trusting people and giving them the benefit of the doubt, but you're good at knowing when someone's trying to pull one over on you. You've got an exceptionally balanced ability to figure out when something isn't quite right, but to also accept things as they are whenever you can. Good for you, smarty!

15-18 points: Super-Cynical

You look at everything with a detective's eye for suspicious details. And while it's good not to believe everything you hear, you might be second-guessing things for no good reason. Try to put some trust in people—you'll find you have more energy left to enjoy life when you're not always scrutinizing it. Trust us.

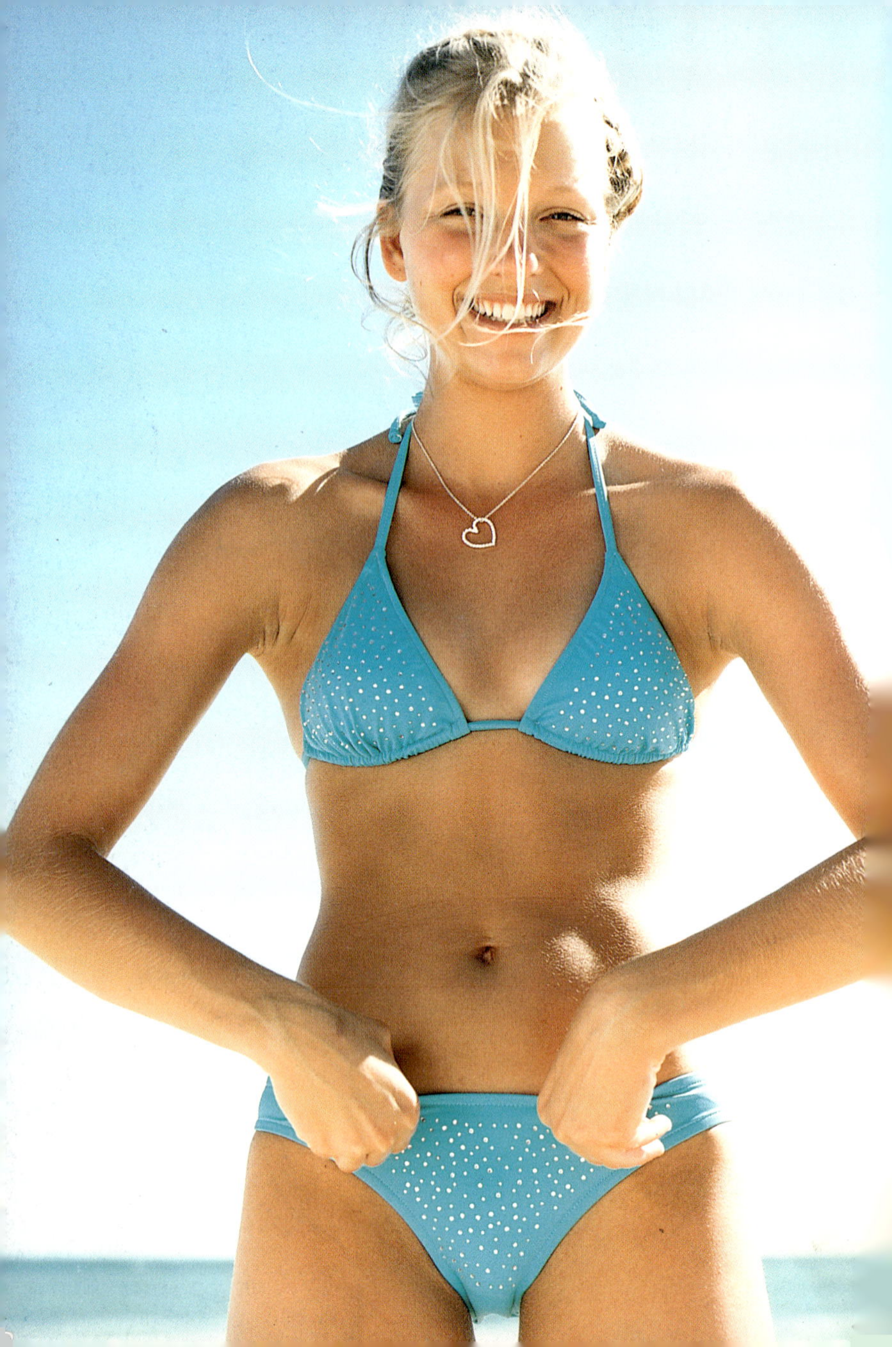

Hear Me Roar

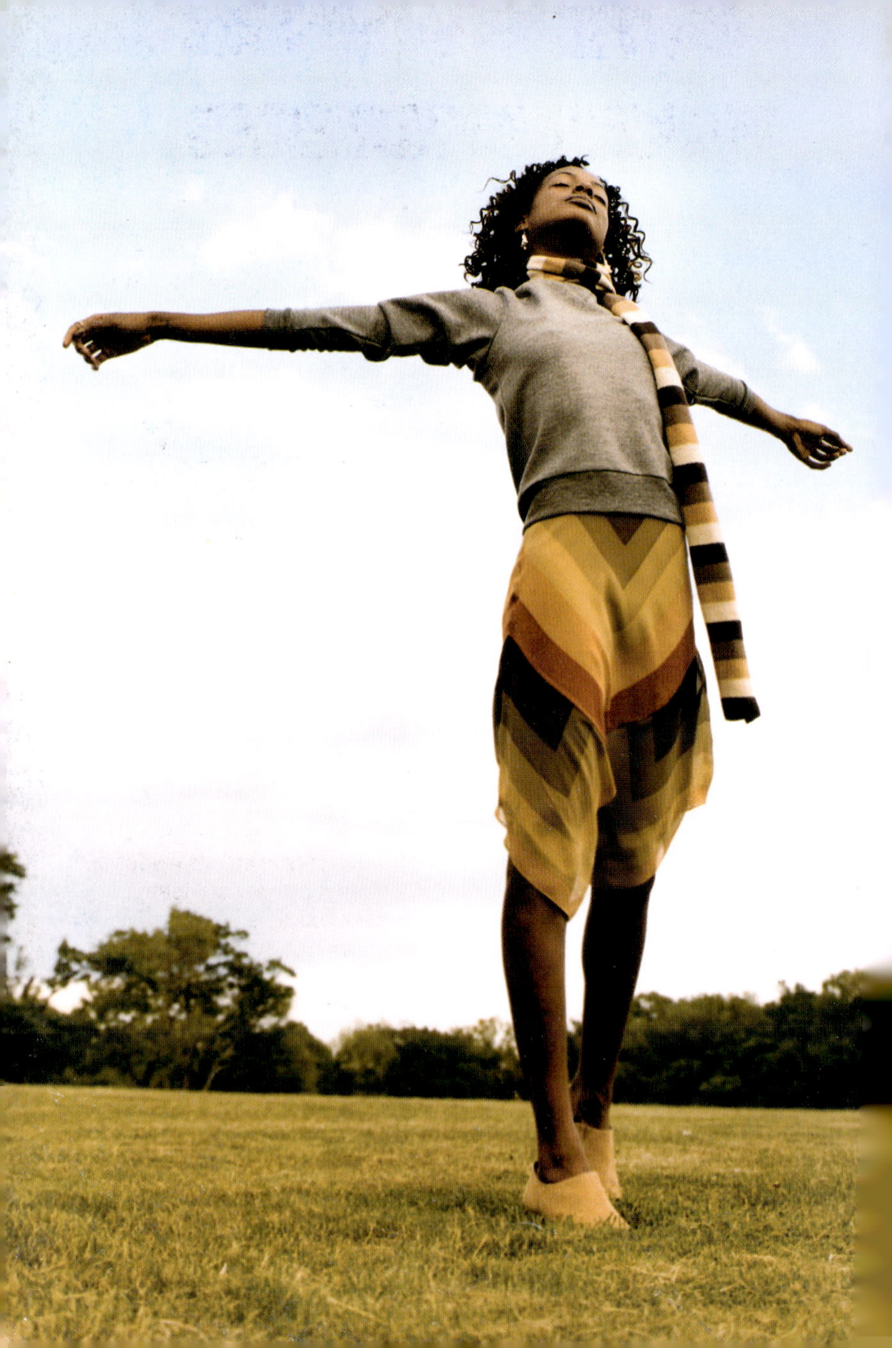

WHO RUNS YOUR LIFE?

Find out if your friends' opinions really matter.

1. You think the new guy in your math class is hot, but your friend says he looks like a loser. You...

a. Think, "To each her own" and then start coming up with ways to ask him out.
b. Wait a few days until you can figure out for yourself whether he's a stud or a dud.
c. Start to reconsider your crush—maybe she has a point and he's not that great.

2. Your friends are raving about the latest Freddie Prinze Jr. flick. You hated it. When they ask you what you thought, you say:

a. "It sucked. I want those hours back!"
b. "It was okay—but not Freddie's best movie. Then again, I'm no Ebert."
c. "It was pretty good. Think about it; anything with Freddie in it can't be that bad."

3. You want to audition for the school play, but your friends are trying to talk you out of it since none of them think it's cool. You...

a. Take the stage without them. You're more determined than ever to snag a role and get to know the theater girls.
b. Do your best to persuade one of your closest friends to audition with you.
c. Stick to things your friends do—maybe next year you'll audition.

4. Your curfew is an hour earlier than everyone else's. You...

a. Try to have as much fun as you possibly can with your friends before you head home on time.
b. Do your best to convince your parents that you deserve that extra sixty minutes of freedom because all your friends have it.
c. Stay out the extra hour anyway and use an excuse that one of your friends comes up with.

5. **You find out that your lab partner stole the answer key to next week's big biology exam. You...**

a. Immediately tell her to trash it—if your teacher questions the class, you will not risk your grade by flat-out lying for her.
b. Do not look at it and try to persuade her to get rid of it before she gets caught.
c. Celebrate your good fortune by treating her to lunch at Taco Bell.

6. **After trying on a million bikinis, you find one that you think looks great. Then your shopping buddy says, "You're not going to buy that, are you?" In return, you say:**

a. "Not only am I going to buy it—I'm planning on wearing it until it falls apart!"
b. "Why? What's wrong with it? I actually thought it was pretty flattering."
c. "No way! I was just joking! Ha-ha."

7. **You're at a party and your favorite can't-help-but-shake-your-groove-thang song comes on. No one is dancing, so you...**

a. Get up and bust a move anyway. Once everyone sees how much fun you're having, chances are they'll join in.
b. Grab your least rhythmically challenged friend by the hand and do everything you can to get her to dance with you.
c. Stay put and start tapping your foot—your friends would mock you for the rest of your life if you danced alone.

SCORING

Mostly a's: MS. INDEPENDENT

The coolest thing about you is that you're not afraid to voice your opinion or try things that others might not. If you like the music, then you'll dance—no matter what all the other wallflowers are doing! Stick to your guns, girl! Your fierce adventurous streak sets you up for opportunities that followers might let pass them by—like the lead role in the school play!

Mostly b's: THOROUGH THINKER

You respect your friends' opinions—but you won't follow advice that you don't agree with. Like with the curfew rule, for instance: You'd never make your parents mad just to make your friends happy. So sometimes you fall in with the crowd, and other times you go solo. Either way, your friends give you props for respecting their right to express themselves—and they respect you even more for knowing when to disagree.

Mostly c's: ALWAYS EAGER TO PLEASE

Your friends mean the world to you. You value their opinions—and usually you're willing to do just about anything for them. But when you ignore your this-isn't-right-for-me radar, you're much more likely to fall into sketchy—or downright dangerous—situations, like getting caught with the stolen exam. So don't be afraid to stand up for what you believe in—friends worth keeping will admire you all the more.

DO YOUR OWN THING
Want to stand your ground? Here's how:
- Recognize the real deal. Only fake friends would ditch you just because of a different point of view—true friends appreciate your unique beliefs. Don't freak out—speak out.
- If you have a different opinion, try to be calm and clear instead of rude or mean.
- Practice being all ears. A plan isn't necessarily bad just because someone else came up with it—so always listen up before deciding what to do.

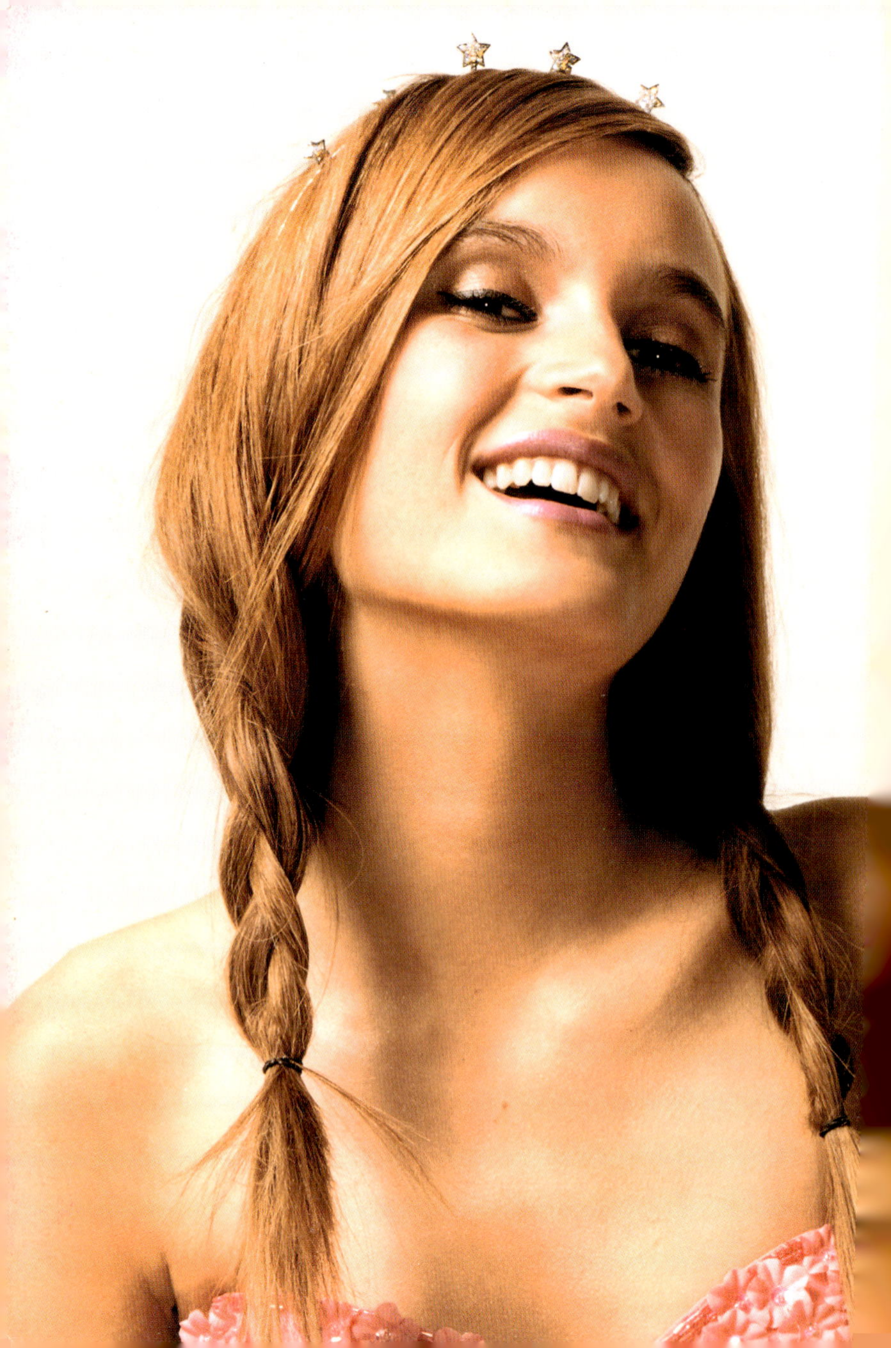

WHAT'S YOUR SECRET POWER?

You've got a hidden talent. Find it—and we'll tell you how to make money off it! Deal?

1. You're in a "good guys vs. bad guys" movie. Which good-guy role would you choose to play?

a. An FBI agent. You love to dissect clues and save the day!
b. An international spy. You'd do your own stunts, thankyouverymuch.
c. A cop (with a heart of gold!). Your gut always leads you to the truth.
d. A prosecutor. You'll make the bad guys play by the rules.

2. If your crush gave you a compliment (and why not? You deserve it!), which one would you be most likely to get?

a. "You're hot, and it's awesome that you're so smart too."
b. "You're hot, and I always have so much fun with you."
c. "You're hot, and you really get me better than anyone else."
d. "You're hot, and you give me the best advice."

3. Okay, admit it (we won't tell a soul!). What's your secret cable-channel addiction?

a. The Discovery Channel
b. The Sci-Fi Channel
c. A&E (love the Biography series!)
d. Lifetime Television

4. At your best friend's party, you're likely to be:

a. Playing a game.
b. Dancing like a wild woman.
c. Having an intense conversation with just a few people.
d. Making yummy hors d'oeuvres.

5. You're doing a group project at school. You:

a. Volunteer to research it. You love surfing the Web.
b. Come up with really creative ways to present the topic to the class.
c. Know who's going to butt heads in the group, and play peacemaker.
d. End up doing most of the work since everyone else usually slacks off!

6. If there's one thing you can't stand, it's when you feel:
a. Like you look dumb.
b. Caged up like a zoo animal.
c. Betrayed by someone you love.
d. As useless as navel lint.

7. Your crush mumbles a message on your answering machine, and you can't understand him. You:
a. Play back the tape over and over and carefully consider the different reasons he might have called.
b. Call him back to find out what he wanted. What've you got to lose?
c. Call your friends and analyze why he might have called you.
d. Think his mumbling means he's nervous around you... which can only signify that he really, really likes you!

ANSWERS:

Mostly a's?

You're a mastermind
Secret Strength: intellect

Words to describe you: logical, strong willed, analytical, innovative

Power profile: You know that saying "knowledge is power"? Well they made it up with you in mind! You're a sharp thinker, and your emotions don't get in the way of your decision making. You like to reflect on any experience to see what you can take away from it—whether it's good or bad. You think, "Okay, what did I learn and how can I use it in the future?" The result? You've got a theory on almost everything—like your "how to tell if a guy likes you" theory, your "when it's okay to break curfew" theory—we could go on! Since you hate passing up opportunities, you tend to overload yourself and get stressed out. But your need to be in control whips you back on track.

How to work it: You're always thinking so fast that before you can put one idea into action, you've moved on to the next one. Make those ideas into success stories by strategizing! First, get yourself a special dream book with folders inside, where you can jot down your interests and ideas and file stuff you find that relates to them. Soon you'll start to see that a basic interest in, let's say, travel might morph into an idea for a teen travel guide. Whatever it is, it jumps out and says, "Pick me! You can do this!" Next: Own your idea. Plot out the steps to making it real (ask a teacher to help you write a book proposal, talk to a travel agent about getting free trips for research), and get started! That little book idea might get you a publishing deal and a nationwide tour! Now, maybe you don't want to write a book. Fine—it's up to you to figure out what you'll do to make that dough. But if you follow this advice, it's only a matter of time before you will!

Dream Jobs: Medical researcher, photojournalist, magazine or newspaper writer, surgeon, psychiatrist, computer programmer, engineer, college professor, lawyer, advertising executive, economist, detective.

Mostly b's?

You're a free spirit
Secret Strength: open-mindedness

Words to describe you: unconventional, daring, adaptable, optimistic

Power profile: Some might call you a rebel, but you prefer "nonconformist." You'd rather follow your whims than follow the dress code, and when Nike came out with that "Just Do It" campaign, you thought they were pitching your personal motto. If the world didn't have people with "it's so crazy it just might work!" ideas like you do, there's no way we'd have cell phones, planes, or Napster. (Thanks!) But since spontaneity is your way of life, you tend to be a tad disorganized (just a tad!). Still, you're a charmer who everyone loves being around and who's known for turning even the most boring situation into a total blast.

How to work it: You can't just wing it when it comes to real success. The trick to making your multimillion-dollar ideas into real multimillions is the follow-through. So rally your entourage (you know, the people who'll be able to say they knew you when), and ask them to stay on your back about that goal you want to go after—whether it's Hollywood stardom or the dog-walking charity fashion show you dreamed up. Get a friend to help you create an action plan, ask another friend for her input, and so on. The more people who see you're serious about meeting this goal, the more people who will ask you if you've made any progress. You won't want to let them down, so you'll be motivated to keep at it. The bottom line? Marry your risk-taking ability with stick-to-itiveness, because as the saying goes, "genius is 1 percent inspiration and 99 percent perspiration." If you follow through, there's no telling how much money you'll rake in. Um, can we have your autograph now?

Dream Jobs: Computer-game designer, fashion editor, novelist, actor, stockbroker, entrepreneur, celebrity publicist, international news reporter, personal trainer, makeup artist, musician, interior designer, master chef.

Mostly c's?

You're a visionary
Secret Strength: intuition

Words to describe you: idealistic, sensitive, articulate, empathetic

Power profile: You're the ultimate people person. With your excellent listening skills, you "hear" what people aren't saying as well as what they are saying. (Psst! Your gut tells you!) You see right through someone who's putting on a happy face when they're dying inside, and you know just how to get them to open up about it and work through it. Because you divide your energy among lots of people (you've got tons of friends), you sometimes end up putting your own goals on the back burner. Still, when you do dream, you dream big because you not only see what is, but what could be and what should be. It's a rare skill to have!

How to work it: How many times have you ignored your instincts and listened to someone else's advice? And how many times have you thought, "I should've gone with my gut!"? Let that be your mantra, girlfriend. Use that amazing intuition to let your own personal truth lead you to your success. The next time you've got some life dilemma and friends give you their input, go spend some time alone to reconnect with yourself. Write down everyone else's thoughts so you have them (after all, their advice doesn't always suck). Then pretend a friend came to you with this same problem. What would you tell her? That first reaction is what you should follow—even if you have to go against the grain. Whether you want to start your own magazine, direct a film, or do anything that makes someone ask,"How are you ever going to do that?" just know you'll find a way. People in high places will be impressed with your faith in yourself and put a nice paycheck behind it!

Dream Jobs: Activist, kindergarten teacher, psychologist, songwriter, defense lawyer, editor-in-chief, public relations executive, sports recruiter, theater director, talent agent, foreign ambassador, fashion photographer.

Mostly d's?

You're a guardian angel
Secret Strength: maturity

Words to describe you: responsible, supportive, organized, devoted

Power profile: Okay, were you born grown up? You're the "put-together"girl who always keeps her head—even if you're having trouble at school, with friends and family, or with guys. You like taking care of details and you don't like wasting time; plus, you secretly feel like you're the only one who can do something right. So it's no wonder that you often find yourself being the plan maker! But by always taking charge, you sometimes end up resenting other people for slacking. Still, you really do love the fact that others feel safe with you around. Taking care of people makes you feel good.

How to work it: First, you've got to learn to let some things go. You don't have to be the one who does everything. But when something is really important to you—say, the planning of the prom—the key is to share the load. It's called delegating, and it's about you being the boss (like the sound of that?) and relying on others to do the individual tasks. By stepping back from the grunt work, you're in a position to make sure everything happens according to your very smart plan. The hard part is giving people orders in a way that doesn't make them feel like they're being bossed around. So instead of saying, "You should do blah-blah," try, "I'm thinking you'd be great at blah-blah!" Then, trust them to come through for you. If you give people stuff they'll be good at, you'll find they're psyched to pitch in. Once you master the skill of harnessing people-power, you'll meet your goals—today and in the future!—much more quickly. And since managing people isn't easy, when you're a pro at it, you'll hear, "Okay, how much do you want to be paid?" Cha-ching!

Dream Jobs: High school teacher, movie producer, tour manager, family physician, counselor, speech pathologist, physical therapist, vet, pharmacist, managing editor, social worker.

WHAT'S YOUR FIGHTING STYLE?

When a battle brews, do you stand your ground or suffer in silence?

1. Your best bud borrowed—and lost—your new sunglasses. You...
a. Don't say anything, but vow to yourself that you'll think twice before letting her borrow anything of yours ever again.
b. Tell her you're upset, but accept her apology and let her buy you a CD.
c. Spread the word to all of your other friends that she totally can't be trusted.

2. You show up at a friend's house at 6 o'clock sharp, but she swears you said you'd be there at 5. It's now 7 p.m. and she's still ranting. You...
a. Apologize (again!). Even though it was a simple misunderstanding, you really hate it when she's mad at you.
b. Tell her to get over it already and that pouting won't turn back the clock.
c. Say that you've had enough, split, and don't return her calls for three days.

3. Your new job at the juice bar comes with one little problem: Your coworker expects you to give free smoothies to all her friends. You...
a. Become a giveaway queen. Who wants to deal with a scary confrontation?
b. Tell her (nicely) that you don't feel comfortable with the freebiefest.
c. Say—loud enough for the manager to hear—"Um, your friend forgot to pay" the next time she offers up a free one.

99

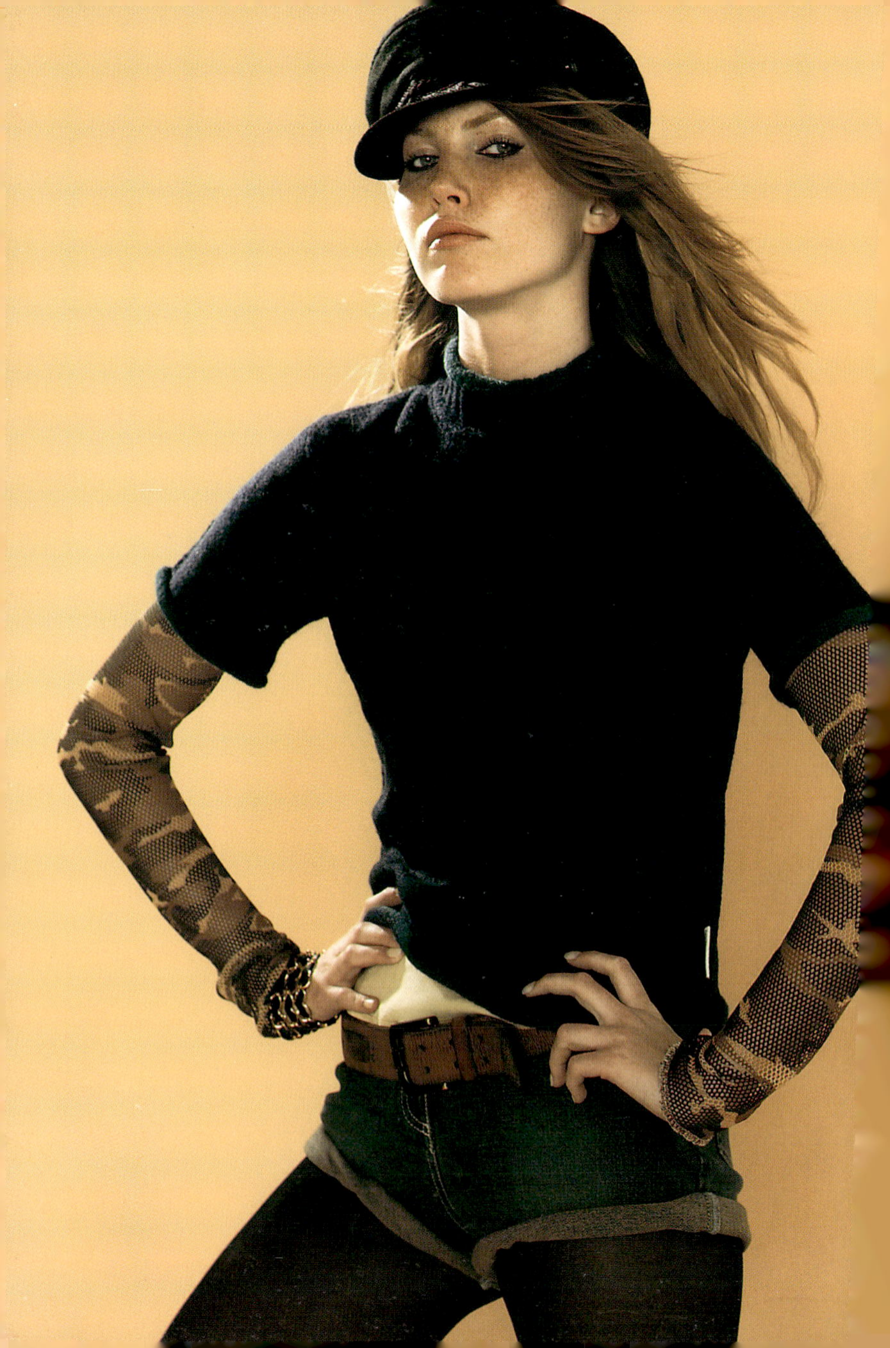

4. Ever since you confessed to a friend about your crush, she hasn't stopped hanging all over him. You let her know you're peeved by...

a. Giving her the silent treatment for a few days. She'll figure out why you're so annoyed with her sooner or later.
b. Asking her flat-out why she's suddenly become his new close friend.
c. Threatening to tell him about her alcoholic dad if she doesn't back off.

5. You fork over a twenty for your combo meal deal, but the cashier only gives you change for a ten. You...

a. Assume you were the one who counted wrong and just let it go.
b. Calmly but firmly point out the error and speak with a manager if you need to.
c. Make a scene and tell everyone around that the cashier is a thief and a liar. You want her to be very sorry for her mistake.

6. Your crush finally calls, but your sister erases the message before you hear it. When you call her on it, she's not exactly apologetic. You...

a. Stomp to your room and fantasize about getting back at her (though you know you won't actually do anything).
b. Tell her point-blank that you've been waiting all week for his call and you're really angry that she erased it.
c. Declare war and erase every one of her messages for the next two weeks.

7. You've been waiting in line all night for concert tickets when the group in front of you lets yet another bunch of their friends cut in front of them. You...

a. Try to catch the eye of the mean-looking guy behind you and hope he's p.o.'d too so he'll kick them out of line.
b. Point out to the cutters that the end of the line is around the corner.
c. Get them booted by yelling "Security! These guys are letting people cut!"

scoring

Give yourself 1 point for every a, 2 for every b, and 3 for every c.

17 to 21 points:

WARRIOR PRINCESS

You're emotional, and you fight to win—even if it means fighting dirty. The next time you get into an argument, take a deep breath and listen to what your "opponent" has to say before blasting into her. After all, what good is winning a fight if you lose a friend (or maybe several)?

12 to 16 points:

FAIR FIGHTER

You keep yourself composed but you're not afraid to express your true feelings—and the facts. Even when someone hits below the belt, you respond calmly and rationally. And because you almost never lose your cool, your friends aren't afraid to tell you when you've done something that really bugged them.

7 to 11 points:

DENIAL QUEEN

Even when you know you should stand your ground, you hate rocking the boat. The next time someone makes you mad, think about exactly what you want to say to that person—then say it! Holding your feelings in will stress you out more, and it could make you resent other people. If you speak up when you're upset—without losing control—friends will respect you, and they might even apologize.

WAGE A WINNING BATTLE
You'll more likely get your way if you:

Stick to the subject. If you say mean things about unrelated issues (like "No wonder your boyfriend cheated on you..."), you'll regret it later. Avoid absolutes. If you say something like, "You never listen to me," you're just setting yourself up to be proven wrong—of course your mom listens to you some of the time! Hear her out. Your opponent needs to know you're listening and not just thinking about your next comeback. So wait until she's finished and then say "I can see your point, but..."

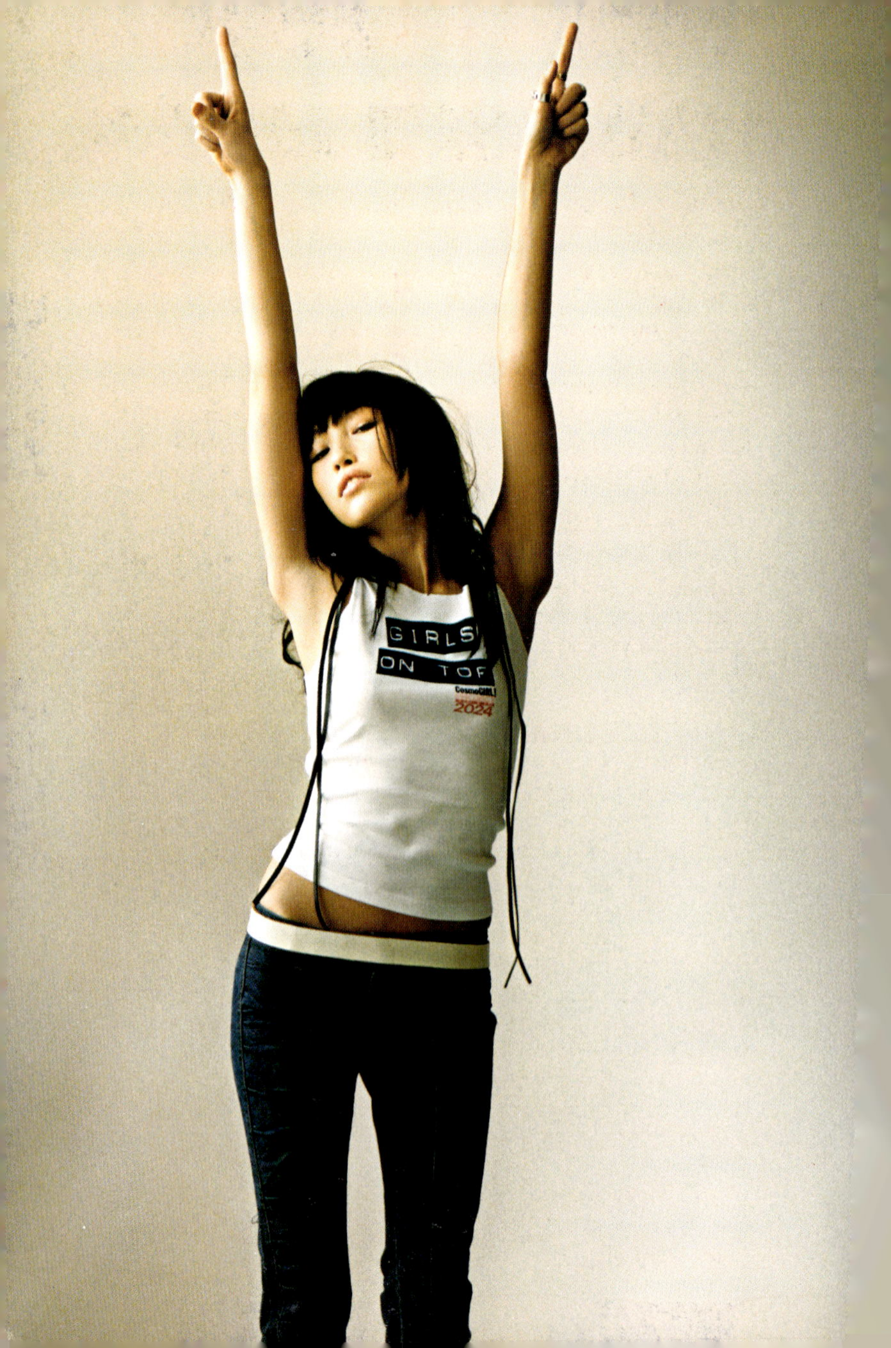
GIRLS
2024

ARE YOU A GOAL GETTER?

Do you control your life, or does it control you?

1. **You have a math test, a paper on the Civil War, and an art project all due the same day. You...**

a. Panic. You'll study for the test and beg your other teachers for an extension.
b. Prioritize. You'll just block off separate times for each assignment.
c. Procrastinate. You'll load up on candy and caffeine the night before and cram. That's how you work best, anyway.

2. **That adorable skater guy you have a crush on smiles at you in the hall. You...**

a. Go to his favorite ramp every day to see him skate (homework, be darned!).
b. Find out his class schedule and "coincidentally" bump into him before lunch.
c. Ask him what he's up to Saturday and make plans to hang out—even if your whole weekend is already booked.

3. **You're dying to go on a trip with a friend's family, but your mom and dad won't pay. So you...**

a. Get a waitressing job. If the tips are lousy, you'll work six shifts a week (even if you have to quit the play).
b. Get a weekend job. A few Saturdays making lattes should earn you just enough cash.
c. Scrounge up cash doing random chores. It'll add up, right?

4. **Your sister's birthday is coming up, and you want to make her a great scrapbook. You'll probably...**

a. Stay up all night to finish it right away even though you have a huge swim meet the next day.
b. Work on it a little every day for a week so that it's ready in time.
c. Get totally overwhelmed and give it to her a week late.

5. **The last time you went shopping for a dress for a school dance, you...**
a. Wanted something very specific and shopped every day for a month until you found it.
b. Found a great dress that went well with your favorite pair of evening shoes.
c. Store-hopped for six hours and blew your cash on dirty denim jeans instead.

6. **Your mom's tired of buying Halloween costumes, so you offer to make one for your little brother. At 3 p.m., October 31, you're...**
a. Arguing with your mom. (She's annoyed you spent more money on the supplies than if you'd just bought the costume.)
b. Finishing up your brother's face paint and sending him out the door.
c. Desperately trying to make something out of an old bedsheet in time.

7. **It's class election time, and you've decided to run for student council. Your campaign strategy:**
a. Spend every minute campaigning, even if it means less time spent with friends.
b. Ask a friend to be campaign manager; the two of you can get all the poster and button making done on weekends.
c. Well, you had some great ideas but you were too busy to make them happen.

SCORING

Mostly a's: SUPER-FOCUSED

You're great at zooming in, but you only focus on one thing at a time. When your mind's set on a goal (like getting a part in the school play or acing a history test), you go too far and either drop everything else in your life or veer away from the original plan. Spread out your super-honing skills by taking on a few projects at once and setting small daily goals. You'll see you really can do it all. Promise.

Mostly b's: GREAT GOALIE

You're great at planning ahead and meeting your goals—whether they're serious (like school) or fun (like making time for friends). Being able to juggle multiple tasks will always help you stay on track—just be sure to plan for some downtime too. Read a book or rent a movie with friends—you'll de-stress and be able to meet your goals even better.

Mostly c's: JUGGLING ACT

You're great at starting projects, but finishing them is another story. You just have too many other exciting things going on at once. If you're tempted to drop something halfway through, focus on getting through to the end. Then reward yourself! Limit yourself to just a few projects at once, and then map out a way to meet your goals. P.S.: If you don't own a planner, get one now!

TOTAL TASKMASTER
To stay on top of your to-dos...
• Be a clock wizard. Time every task for a week (from reading a chapter of history to washing the dishes). Then use that info to help you plan in the future. Make a "time map." Color code your planner with blocks of time (red for school, blue for friends, etc.). Just say no. Before you take on a new project, ask yourself: How will this help me? If you don't know, let it go.

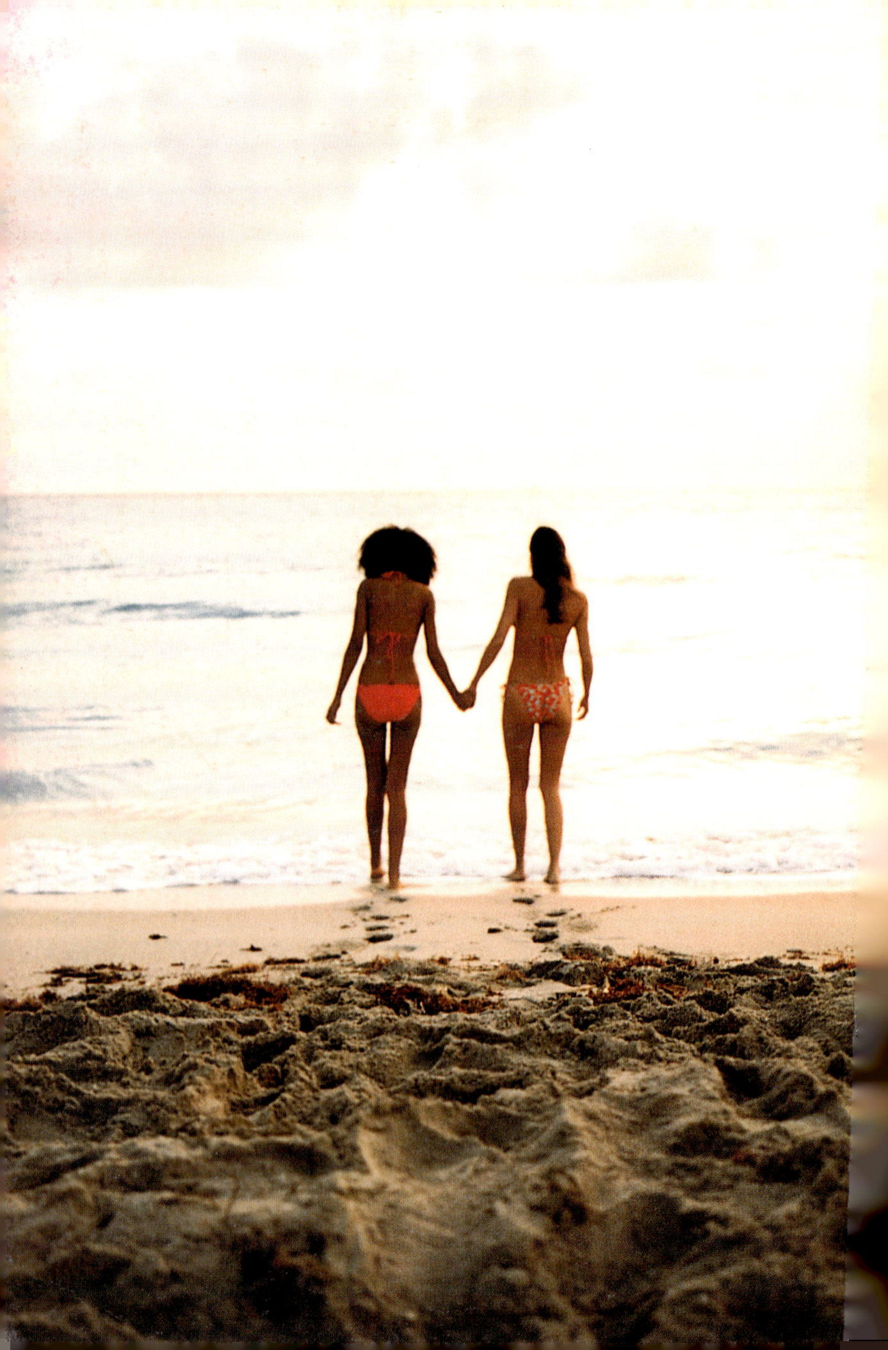

ARE YOU A LEADER?

Find out if your friends look up to you—or look back to make sure you're there.

1. You and your girls are planning a surprise birthday party for a friend. You immediately:

a. Start organizing who's going to take care of invitations, gifts, decorations, snacks, etc.
b. Say, "Does anyone mind if I play DJ? I have a couple of really good mixes in mind."
c. Go, "Let me know what I need to do"—and then do what they tell you.

2. Your group wants to give old clothes to Goodwill, but no one's sure how to get them there. You:

a. Figure out a day that's convenient to stop by each one's house so you can fill your trunk and get it done in one big haul.
b. Offer to drop it all off—if they'll just bring what they have to your house.
c. Wait for someone else to figure out what you guys need to do.

3. You're in the hall when a new girl trips and drops her books all over the place. You:

a. Smile at her, walk over, and help her pull her stuff together.
b. Smile sympathetically but help her only if someone else does first!
c. Think, She must be so embarrassed.

4. On the first day of driver's ed, your teacher asks the class to introduce themselves. You:

a. Raise your hand and say, "I'm Jen, and I'm here to learn to drive stick."
b. Make eye contact and smile at her so she knows that if she needs a volunteer, you're willing to go first.
c. Look down and hope that someone else in the class speaks up soon.

5. One friend of yours always makes plans but then doesn't show up. You deal with it by:

a. Saying you feel like she's been blowing you off lately and asking her to be more considerate.
b. Only inviting her to group activities so her absence won't ruin any plans.
c. Shrugging it off. What can you really do about it anyway?

6. At the movies, some friends want to see a comedy while the rest are big on a drama. You say:

a. "I'd rather watch the comedy later on video—I'll see the drama if anyone wants to come with."
b. "Why don't we take a vote? Or we could just split up and all meet after and do something."
c. "Really, I'm fine with either."

7. Two friends tell you and another friend that they're ditching class to go shopping. You:

a. Say, "No thanks—I don't want to have to play catch-up later."
b. Say, "Maybe next time. I have a quiz today"—even if you don't.
c. Do whatever your friend decides to.

scoring
Give yourself 1 point for every a, 2 for every b, and 3 for every c. Now add 'em up!

7-11 points

first lady

Your friends think you're a bold girl, but the real word for you is leader! You're not freaked by being first, because you see the big picture. Instead of "What will they think of me?" you ask, "How can I help make this happen?" So take your talents beyond just your social circle. Apply them to a school or community group, and we'll see you at the top!

12-16 points
independent woman
If others are more impassioned about something than you are, you'll step back, but if you have a strong opinion, you're not afraid to speak up. To become a better leader, study a friend who does it well. How does she approach people? How does she balance her opinion with others'? Use her lessons in your life, and you'll be team captain soon too!

17-21 points
group thinker
Your friends love that you're always willing to join in on their plans. The only problemo? You may do things you don't want to—just to get along with others. Next time you think, I wish we were doing this instead, say it! You might be outvoted, but either way, saying what's on your mind earns you respect.